Love Seeks No Boundaries

Love Seeks No Boundaries

Sourabh Khanna

Notion Press

5 Muthu Kalathy Street, Triplicane,
Chennai - 600 005

First Published by Notion Press 2014

Copyright © Sourabh Khanna 2014

All Rights Reserved.

ISBN: 978-93-83808-94-6

This book has been published in good faith that the work of the author is original. All efforts have been taken to make the material error-free. However, the author and the publisher disclaim the responsibility.

No part of this book may be used, reproduced in any manner whatsoever without written permission from the author, except in the case of brief quotations embodied in critical articles and reviews.

Dedicated to my family and friends

Acknowledgment

First of all, I would like to pay my gratitude to my family and especially to my father Mr. Harish Khanna, who always support me and stood by me. Secondly, I would like to thank my friends who helped me and motivated me to share my feelings. I won't be able to craft my feelings on a piece of paper and share it without the help of my friends. Lastly, I would like to thank notion press staff and especially to my project manager, you were very supportive and helpful throughout publication process.

Love Seeks No Boundaries

In India there are many religions and castes that follow their own sets of beliefs and rituals – but this wasn't what God intended. He didn't create religion or caste; these were created by people like us.

The beliefs have been engrained in Indian culture, and passed down from one generation to the next, such that some Indians have no choice but to follow. However, how long should one follow and recite the teachings that were passed down, when one knows that the most important thing is humanity? One has to look at everyone equally – only then one will find happiness. However, in India, it is impossible to quell the backward thinkers who know only one way, and who do not care for humanity. These people give more importance to the religion and caste into which they are born. India will never experience change unless someone is willing to go beyond religion and caste.

Sukhi was 22 years old when he moved to Sydney, Australia, and had lived there for six years. He was born into the Brahmin caste, which, in India, is believed to be the highest-ranked caste of all. Sukhi was 5'10", and usually wore formal clothes, but his French-cut beard added a funky touch to his professional look.

On several occasions, Sukhi had encountered religion and caste issues, but had managed to avoid involvement. Never one to follow or believe in the system, he was always ready to lend a helping hand to those in need. Although he strongly believed in the equality of all humanity, his faith in God was just as strong – which led him to recite prayers – but he never indulged in controversial issues. He had many friends who admired him and stood by his ideologies and thoughts, and they were all from different religions and castes.

His family lived in America and had been there for 12 years. Although Sukhi desperately wanted to live closer to them, he couldn't because of priorities that had led him to Australia in the first place. He worked as an account manager at Woolworths, one of the largest supermarket chains in Australia.

On a Monday morning, before he went to work, Sukhi went to McCafe (which was a part of McDonalds) to get a mochacinno. While waiting for his coffee, he looked around and his glance fell on a beautiful Indian girl who was standing behind the counter and taking orders from customers. She was tall and beautiful, with long, black, curly hair, and a small mole on her lower lip.

From her uniform, it was clear that she was the restaurant manager. Sukhi couldn't stop staring at her, but she didn't notice as it was a busy morning. Sukhi had never seen such a beautiful girl in his life before. As she took orders from customers, the girl smiled a lot, which Sukhi found very attractive.

Sukhi's coffee was ready; a counter staff named Amanda called his name to give him his coffee, but Sukhi was busy smiling at the Indian girl. It was as if no one else existed at that moment. Amanda gave the coffee to her co-worker to pass it to him. The staff shook Sukhi's arm and handed over the cup. Sukhi took his coffee and went outside, still looking at the Indian girl. When he reached his workplace, he was still thinking about her, as he had never seen anyone as beautiful as her. Before lunch, he wanted to meet her again.

At lunch time, he went to McDonalds to look for the girl. He ordered some food – which he didn't even want as he didn't like McDonalds. While waiting for his order, he looked for the girl but couldn't find her anywhere. Maybe she was busy at the back. As she was wearing a restaurant manager's uniform, he assumed that she might be doing managerial duties at the back. His order was now ready at the counter, and another staff member yelled out his coupon number.

Sukhi took his food and went outside but his eyes were still searching for her. Unfortunately, he couldn't find her anywhere near the counter, so he returned to his office with the McDonalds bag in hand. He gave the bag to one of his co-workers named Mike, as he hated McDonalds and usually brought lunch from home.

When Sukhi finished work that day, he went to the McDonalds again, parked his car and started to look for the same Indian girl at the counter. He badly wanted to see her – at least to make sure that he was not mistaken.

Unluckily for him, he couldn't find her anywhere in or outside the store; he waited there for an hour, but there was no sign of her. So, he went back to his apartment. He spent the whole evening thinking of that girl. He wanted to meet her and tell her how strongly he felt about her. Then, he wondered if she was single or not. In the end, he convinced himself that she was single and that he would meet her and share his thoughts and feelings.

The next morning, while driving past the McDonalds, he waited at the car park for about five minutes, then went inside to get himself a coffee and to look for the girl. While ordering his coffee, he was stammering and kept looking here and there. Despite his efforts, which caused many people to stare at him, he couldn't see her. He took his coffee and went to office, with a plan to visit McDonalds at lunch time.

During lunch, Sukhi went to McDonalds with Mike. While Mike ordered his food, Sukhi was busy looking around for the girl, but he couldn't find her. He was so upset that he left the place without even waiting for Mike to get his lunch.

Mike came back to office with his lunch, but he was angry at Sukhi for leaving him behind. He wanted to share something with Sukhi, but the latter was not even listening to him.

Mike told him that he had seen an Indian girl there, and that she was very beautiful, but Sukhi didn't even listen as he was still lost in dreams about wanting to see her again. Mike shook his shoulder and asked him if he was listening or not, but Sukhi shook his head and said he was not feeling well and walked back to his cabin.

When they finished work, Mike went to Sukhi's cabin and asked him why he was acting so weird since morning. Sukhi just said he had a headache but that he would be okay soon. Mike asked him to go to his place for drinks, but Sukhi refused as he wanted to have some time alone.

Sukhi then went to the car park of McDonalds and waited there for an hour, unfortunately he didn't see her that time as well. Feeling very sad, he went back to his apartment. While he was driving back to his apartment he was lost in dreams of that mystery girl whose name he didn't even know. He called her "Dream Girl".

Whenever Sukhi closed his eyes, the girl's face and her lovely smile came before him, but he was driving so he kept closing and opening his eyes to feel her presence. He was so lost in thought that he crossed his apartment building and continued to drive ahead.

Only when he was very far away from his apartment did he realise that he was lost, and that he was driving on a highway that led to another city. He then took the first exit that came his way and made a U-turn so that he could get back home.

When he reached his apartment, he was smiling at his imagination. This was the first time he had felt something for a girl – a new feeling, as he had always maintained a distance from girls.

Sukhi continued to go to McDonalds to look for that girl for the next two weeks, but he didn't see her. He became upset and made up his mind to stop looking for her and focus on his career.

One day, during his break time at work, he went to the security room to look for Mike. Mike wasn't there, but out of the blue Sukhi's eyes stopped on the CCTV and he was surprised to see the same girl whom he was searching for so long. She was shopping downstairs in the store, but she was accompanied by a tall guy. Sukhi was disappointed, but he wanted to see her closely so he went down to the store and pretended to check some barcodes in one of the aisles. He was stalking her through the aisle gaps and he couldn't stop himself from chasing her through each and every aisle they went into.

The girl was not in the McDonalds uniform, and Sukhi found it difficult to talk to her. Suddenly, she and her friend came to the same aisle that Sukhi was standing in; her friend called Sukhi and asked him for a particular brand of yoghurt. Sukhi told him to wait for a while so that he could look for it in the storeroom.

While Sukhi was going in the storeroom, the two of them started following him to the storeroom and at one point they were talking about some chicken soup. Then the guy addressed the girl as 'Priya'. When Sukhi heard that, he smiled, for he now knew her name.

Sukhi told them to wait outside the storeroom so that he could go inside and look for the yoghurt. He went into the storeroom but couldn't find what he was looking for. So, he went back and told them that the particular yoghurt was out of stock and that he would let the manager know.

Priya and her friend were disappointed and went back to their shopping list to look for other stuff to buy. Sukhi saw Priya's face fall when he told them that he couldn't find their yoghurt, and he felt very bad. So he asked another staff to look for the same yoghurt – just so that he could put the smile back on Priya's face.

The other staff member came back with the same brand of yoghurt that they wanted, and Sukhi went in search of Priya in the store. He saw her by the frozen foods aisle. He gathered his guts, went to her, and said, "Excuse me".

"Yes," Priya replied with a smile.

Sukhi paused for a few seconds and said, "I found your yoghurt".

"Yippee!" she shouted and smiled.

Sukhi gave her the yoghurt and turned away. After couple of seconds, he heard a sweet, soft voice saying, "Excuse me, sir". Sukhi turned and saw Priya smiling at him. She thanked him and Sukhi replied, "It's my pleasure, miss". They were smiling at each other until she went outside.

The next day, Sukhi woke up early. He couldn't sleep properly because he kept dreaming about Priya, and was a bit jealous as she was accompanied by her male friend in the dream – and it appeared that she might be committed to him. This made Sukhi feel very insecure – he couldn't be with her as she might not want to be with anyone else if she was committed to that guy.

He didn't want to face that possibility, so he decided to let the fantasy go and return to life as it was before her.

But sometimes, destiny has something else planned for you and you have no control over it. Sukhi's destiny had also planned something else, which he was not aware of.

When Sukhi was on the way to work, he wanted to get coffee but didn't want to go to McCafe. So, he went to Starbucks instead, but the place was packed with customers. To avoid being delayed for work, he half-heartedly went to McCafe and ordered a coffee.

While waiting for his coffee, Sukhi was reading the newspaper. He heard someone talking, so he looked up – his jaw dropped when he saw Priya taking orders from customers. He had made up his mind not to go after her, but his heart was beating hard and he ended up staring at her.

This time, Priya noticed that Sukhi was staring at her and she felt uncomfortable and angrily looked back at him. Sukhi shook his head and started looking elsewhere, but, after sometime, she caught him staring at her again. This time, she looked even angrier. Sukhi was embarrassed, so he looked down and avoided looking at her while waiting for his coffee. Priya smiled at his innocent reaction, but he didn't notice it.

When his coffee was ready, Sukhi took it and left. He didn't have the courage to look at Priya, so he rushed to his car. Priya, who was watching him, just shook his head and mumbled, "Mad guy!"

Sukhi was very disappointed when he realised that Priya was not interested in him. He went to his cabin and started doing his work, but completely forgot about a meeting with his boss, Kevin. He was sitting in his cabin, head bent over the table, when his boss came and stood around for about five minutes.

Sukhi didn't even realise that Kevin was standing next to him. When he looked up and saw Kevin there, he realised that he had a meeting that he had forgotten to attend. He stood up and apologised for his negligence. Kevin told Sukhi to come to his cabin in five minutes. After Kevin left, Sukhi breathed a sigh of relief and drank some water before going to Kevin's office. When he knocked on the door, his boss answered, "Yes, come in Sukhi". Sukhi went inside and Kevin told him to sit down, and asked him why he had forgotten to attend the meeting.

Sukhi apologised and said that he had even prepared everything the previous day, but had completely forgotten about it. He assured Kevin that it would never happen again and handed over all the files.

Kevin said, "Can I ask you something?"

"Yeah sure, Kevin," Sukhi replied.

"Are you not happy working here?" Kevin asked. Sukhi replied with a smile that he loved working there and that he was not looking for a job elsewhere. Kevin said that he needed Sukhi there and that he didn't want to lose him at any cost. Sukhi apologised again, and assured Kevin that his work would be on track.

Sukhi returned to his cabin, but he felt very disappointed and cursed himself for having a bad day. He was back on the chair, and rested his head on the table. All of sudden, Mike came over and asked Sukhi what the matter was. Sukhi explained everything to Mike, and said he might be in love with a girl he had seen.

Mike jumped up in joy because he knew that Sukhi had never been in any relationships so far – now was his chance to get to know someone. When Sukhi told him about the guy he had seen with Priya, Mike's face fell but he promised to introduce Sukhi to some others he knew. Sukhi said that he didn't feel fine at that moment as he had been had a talk with Kevin about the meeting. Mike told him not to worry, and asked Sukhi to go over to his place in the evening for drinks. He also promised Sukhi that he would introduce him to some of his female friends.

That evening, when Sukhi went to Mike's place, the house was full of people. Many of his co-workers were there as well. Sukhi felt uncomfortable at first, but, after sometime, as Mike introduced him to his friends, he felt much better.

After a while, Sukhi took a drink and stood in a corner, lost in thoughts about Priya. Mike saw Sukhi standing by himself, and went over to talk to him. Mike stood next to Sukhi and handed over another drink. Sukhi told him that he would be leaving soon as he couldn't take his mind off that girl and he was feeling a bit uncomfortable. Mike understood that Sukhi was heartbroken, and he wanted to cheer him up. He told Sukhi to stick around for a little while as he had a surprise for him.

Just then, someone knocked on the door, and Mike asked Sukhi to open it. Sukhi said Mike should go as it would be his friends and he had to receive them, but Mike said he needed to go to the toilet. So, Sukhi went to open the door. There was a beautiful girl standing outside. She was tall and good looking and, even before he said anything, she said, "So, you must be Sukhi!" Sukhi was shocked and surprised at the same time. How did she know his name? Then Mike came up introduced them to each other. The girl's name was Courtney and she was a friend of Mike's girlfriend.

Courtney then asked Mike in a whisper if this was the same guy he had mentioned over the phone. Mike nodded, and then Courtney whispered that he seemed to be a nice guy. Mike again nodded and smiled, and told them to hang around with each other as he had to attend some other guests as well. Before Sukhi could refuse, he had left, so Sukhi had to stick with Courtney.

Sukhi wondered if Courtney was the 'surprise' that Mike was telling him about. He stood next to her quietly, while she wondered how to start a conversation. She began by saying that her name was Courtney and that she was from Melbourne, but had shifted to Sydney a couple of months back. Sukhi just smiled in response, but she kept on talking.

After a couple of minutes, Sukhi interrupted her and said he would get her a drink and that they could go to the balcony after. Courtney raised her eyebrows and said that she was impressed with his cordial behaviour, and agreed. Sukhi got her a drink and they went to the balcony.

Mike's apartment was in the heart of the city, and they could see the whole city and beautiful lighting of the Opera House from the balcony. Before she could say anything, Sukhi told Courtney that she looked nice. Courtney smiled and replied that she found it very hard to believe he was single since he was such a nice guy and smart too. Sukhi sipped his drink and replied that Mike was also a nice guy, and he knew that Mike was the one who was trying to set them up.

Courtney was very impressed with Sukhi's innocent and warm nature, so she asked for his phone number, which Sukhi gave. They both sipped their drinks and talked for an hour before Mike interrupted them to call them for dinner. Courtney wanted to leave as she had some other things to do, but Mike insisted that she could stay for a while and go after dinner. She refused, but when Sukhi asked her to stay, she agreed and they smiled at each other. Mike was very happy as Sukhi seemed to be interested in Courtney.

After dinner, when Courtney was leaving, Mike went up to her and asked about how it went with Sukhi. Courtney smiled and replied that she would think about it after Sukhi called her, as she had already given her number to him. Mike then went to Sukhi and asked him the same question, but Sukhi said that he was not sure about Courtney as he couldn't get rid of Priya from his mind. Mike told him that Priya might be committed to someone else – maybe the same guy Sukhi saw her with at the supermarket. He asked Sukhi to at least give it a try with Courtney as she might be a turning point in Sukhi's life and help him to forget about Priya. Sukhi then put his head down and told Mike that he would think about Courtney, but right now he needed some time to get over Priya. Mike was happy with that response and wished him luck.

Sukhi went to his apartment and lay down on his couch, thinking about Priya, when, all of sudden, he thought of a solution – he switched on his laptop and opened his Facebook page to search for her. He typed 'Priya' in the search column, and was astonished to see that there were so many profiles with the same name. He went through each and every profile that showed up and, after sometime, thought of narrowing it down. He typed 'Priya' and 'Sydney' in the search column, but still couldn't find her on Facebook. He was disappointed, so he angrily switched off his laptop and went to bed.

At around 3 a.m., Sukhi woke up. He was unable to sleep as he kept thinking of Priya. He got up and went to the bathroom, and, while washing his hands, looked into the mirror – he was shocked to see Priya standing behind him while he was looking in the mirror but when he turned his face to see her, there was no one standing there. Sukhi was mad at himself for imagining Priya everywhere he looked, so he made himself a drink and went to bed again.

The next morning, he was feeling restless as he didn't sleep well. While on his way to work, he decided to go to McDonalds again to grab a coffee, but before he went inside he looked for Priya because he didn't want to act desperate in front of her. He didn't find her anywhere; instead of going in, he started his car and drove to his workplace.

When he went to work, he saw Mike standing outside, having a smoke. Mike asked Sukhi how he was. Sukhi just nodded and went inside. Mike finished his smoke and went to Sukhi's cabin and asked him what the matter was. Sukhi told him that he couldn't even sleep properly as Priya kept coming in his dreams now and that he desperately wanted to see her. Mike said, "Why don't we go to McDonalds and get ourselves a coffee?" Sukhi was surprised as Mike hated coffee. Mike said he would drink anything for Sukhi; they smiled and headed to McDonalds.

They went inside the café and stood around talking about work. Mike ordered the coffee and stood there for a while so that Sukhi could look through the window for Priya. But Sukhi couldn't see her anywhere. While Sukhi and Mike were chatting about their work, they heard a sweet, soft voice saying, "Excuse me". Sukhi knew it was Priya's voice and turned around. Sukhi smiled at her, but she didn't smile back. Instead, she rudely told him to step aside as she needed to fill up the tissue rack on the shelf against which they were leaning. Sukhi apologised and moved aside.

While Sukhi was being insulted by his 'dream girl', their coffee was also ready at the counter. Mike grabbed the coffee and went outside with Sukhi. Mike had seen Priya for the first time; he also thought that she was very beautiful and complemented Sukhi's choice. Sukhi smiled at him and took his coffee, and they began to walk towards their workplace. However, on the way back, Mike teased Sukhi about being insulted by his 'dream girl'. He told him that there was no chance of Priya being interested in him, and asked him to concentrate on Courtney. Sukhi was irritated and told Mike to shut up and walk quietly. They reached their workplace and went to their cabins.

At around lunch time, Mike went to Sukhi's cabin and asked him if he was ready for lunch or not. Sukhi told him to wait for a little while as he was in the middle of some important work, and he had to finish it as soon – if not, the payment would be stuck for two days. Mike said he would wait for him, but Sukhi asked him to go ahead.

After some time, when Sukhi went to the staff room, he saw that Mike had actually waited for him. Sukhi looked at him and smiled. While they were having lunch, Sukhi was quiet and Mike was observing his behaviour. After lunch, Mike couldn't resist asking Sukhi what had happened to him, as he had seemed happy at his place last night.

Sukhi refused to say anything. Then Mike told him to go and talk to Priya – he didn't like Sukhi's behaviour; maybe after he approached Priya, he might be happy and normal as he was before. But Sukhi said that talking to her might not be a good idea. Moreover, she might be committed to someone else. Mike got irritated and shouted at Sukhi to forget about Priya and concentrate on Courtney, as he couldn't stand Sukhi being quiet and sad. Sukhi didn't like the idea of being attached to Courtney, and told Mike that he would think about it later. Sukhi also added that he didn't have anything against Courtney, but he wouldn't be able to give her the respect and love she might expect.

While they were talking, Mike's cell phone beeped – it was a text message from Courtney. She wrote that Sukhi seemed like a nice guy and that she was happy to go out with him. Mike showed Sukhi the message, but Sukhi was still sad. It appeared that he couldn't even think of anyone else at that moment and he wanted to live in his dreams of Priya. Sukhi got up and went to his cabin; Mike was left alone, surprised at how bad Sukhi was feeling.

When he finished work, Sukhi went to Mike's cabin to apologise for his behaviour, but Mike had already left. When he was driving back to his apartment, Sukhi couldn't resist going to McDonalds to stalk Priya for the last time. He decided to move on with his life, so he wanted to see Priya one last time. Unfortunately, it was not in his destiny to see her, so he started his car and drove to his apartment.

When he was home, he decided to call Courtney for dinner as he really wanted to move on. After some thought, he messaged Courtney and asked her to dinner at his place if she was not busy. Courtney called him back and said she was not busy, and that she would be there for dinner. So Sukhi went to freshen up and prepare dinner.

When Courtney came to his place, she was amazed by how tidy his place was, and by the fragrance of the food. She asked him why he didn't text her earlier. Sukhi said he had been busy with something and that he didn't have time to text her. He added that he had thought of texting her but had stopped himself as she might be busy in her work.

The dinner table was set in the balcony; the view was very nice from there. Sukhi had taken up the apartment just for the view. Sukhi had even set out a candle and some wine glasses on the table. Courtney looked at him and said she was impressed with the decoration and preparation for the dinner. Sukhi smiled and appreciated the fact that she came for the dinner.

After dinner, they sat on the couch in the living room and talked about their life and families. After some time, Courtney wanted to leave as it was getting late; Sukhi didn't stop her as he thought she really wanted to go. At the door, Sukhi asked her if he could drop her home. Courtney smiled and agreed, so Sukhi quickly grabbed his car keys and went down to the car park with her. While they were driving, Courtney thanked him for a lovely evening at his place, and added that she really enjoyed his company. Sukhi smiled and said he also enjoyed her company.

While driving back home after dropping Courtney, Sukhi was shocked to see Priya on the other side of the road, walking alongside the same guy from the store. They were holding hands. Sukhi felt very sad, but he was happy for Priya as she looked very happy. Now Sukhi was sure that Priya was already committed to that guy. He had to move on in his own life, and remove Priya from his thoughts.

Next day, when he reached his workplace, he saw Mike standing outside for a smoke and he stopped to talk to him. Mike asked him where his coffee was; Sukhi smiled and said he didn't need it as he had slept well last night. When they were walking to their cabins, Sukhi told Mike that he had been with Courtney last night and that they had had dinner together.

Mike was shocked and asked him to repeat his words. Sukhi replied with a smile and said he had had dinner with Courtney at his place. Mike jumped with joy and said he was happy that Sukhi had finally moved on from Priya. Sukhi replied that he had not committed to Courtney yet. He wanted to give it a try as he was feeling lonely – that's why he called Courtney for dinner.

Sukhi added that apart from dinner they talked about each other's interests, and he was surprised that they had a lot in common like in music and video games, and that she had collected more games and movies than him. Sukhi also told him to not to get his hopes up as he was not sure if he wanted to move on with Courtney or not. Mike hugged him and said he just wanted him to be happy.

At lunch time, Sukhi went to Mike's cabin. Mike was on the phone, so Sukhi asked him to lunch through gestures. Mike said he was busy with a client, so Sukhi would have to wait for a while. Sukhi replied that Mike could take his time and that he would wait. On the way to the staffroom, Mike teased Sukhi asking if they should go to McDonalds to get lunch. Sukhi replied angrily that if Mike wanted to go there, he had to go alone. Mike apologised but said he was serious as he had forgotten his lunch at home; he begged Sukhi to go along with him. Sukhi half-heartedly agreed and they headed to McDonalds.

When they entered the McDonalds, Mike went to the counter, ordered a meal and went back to where Sukhi was standing. Mike was talking to him, but Sukhi was not listening as he was looking at Priya. She was helping a colleague load apple pies into the warmer.

Sukhi continued to stare at her like no one else existed there. Mike told Sukhi to stop staring as the other staff members were beginning to notice. When Sukhi looked up, Mike was shocked to see tears in Sukhi's eyes. He held Sukhi's hand and told him to let her go as she was committed to someone else.

Sukhi told Mike he would go outside and wait in the car park. After some time, Mike took his lunch and went to join Sukhi. They started walking towards their workplace, and Mike kept telling him that he had to put Priya out of his mind as she was already committed to someone else. He added, "It's not worth it, bro." Sukhi apologised and said he had gotten carried away at McDonalds. Mike said he was always with him and he didn't have to say sorry for anything and if he needed any help, he would be there at any time and at any place. He made Sukhi promise him that the latter would forget about Priya.

When Sukhi was working in his cabin, he kept imagining about Priya. He felt helpless. So, he decided that when he finished work, he would go over and talk to her about his feelings. But he was also worried that she might think that he was crazy. So he decided to move on and think of Courtney.

When he finished work, he again went to the McDonald's car park, but didn't get down from his car. He looked for Priya through the glass, but he couldn't see her anywhere near the counter. So he drove to his apartment.

Back home, to divert his attention, he switched on the TV to watch a movie or the news, but his mind was still at the McDonalds. He grabbed his laptop and searched for Priya on Facebook. This time, he narrowed his search for Priya from Sydney who worked at McDonalds. There were a few profiles under that name and profession, so he went through each and every profile.

While he was looking through the profiles, he saw a photo that matched Priya so he opened up that profile – he was astonished that it was her profile and he jumped with joy. He started looking through her pictures but most of them were locked. Those that were not locked didn't have any pictures of the guy with whom she came to the supermarket. He went to the "About Me" section, but the relationship status, which he desperately wanted to see, was not shown. He called Mike and told him that he had found Priya on Facebook but the relationship status was not shown. Mike got upset that Sukhi was trying going to change his feelings for Priya, but later suggested that Sukhi send her a friend request and wait for the reply.

Sukhi was worried that it might make a bad impression on her, but Mike said it was fine to send a friend request as it would be a baby step for him, and, if she was single, she would have no problem accepting the request. Excited, Sukhi send her a friend request. After every half-hour, he checked his notifications to see if she had responded or not.

Sukhi waited for a reply the whole night but got nothing out of it except disappointment and embarrassment.

His hopes of getting close to her were shattered, and he could only blame himself about his stupidity for sending her a friend request. He struggled to get some sleep; in the end, he got up and grabbed a drink and went then back to the bed.

The next morning, he was feeling restless but somehow got ready for work. When he was driving to his work he drove through another way to work as he didn't want to stop at McDonalds and was scared to face Priya. When he got to work, Mike was standing outside, waiting for him. He was surprised to see Sukhi coming from a different way, but didn't get a proper reply when he asked Sukhi about it. Mike knew that something was wrong, so he asked him again why he had taken a different route. Sukhi replied that he didn't want to stop at McDonalds, so he chose to come to work from that way.

Sukhi was a bit rude, yet Mike politely asked him what had happened to him. Sukhi said that Priya hadn't replied to him yet and that's why he was upset and bit worried too. Mike said she might not have checked her Facebook account. "So, there is no big deal. Cheer up!" Mike said, but Sukhi didn't listen.

At lunch time, Mike knocked on Sukhi's cabin door. Sukhi smiled and asked him to come in. Mike sat down next to him and said that they were going to McDonalds. But Sukhi was not keen as he thought Priya was probably angry with him, and he was scared to face her. Mike told him not to worry, as she wouldn't kill him for sending her a friend request. Also, it was never said that if he sent her a friend request, he had no right to go to McDonalds so Mike forcefully convinced Sukhi to go with him.

Sukhi followed Mike to the McDonalds. Mike went inside, but Sukhi stayed outside. After Mike ordered his food, he looked back to ask Sukhi if he wanted anything, and saw him standing outside. Mike gave his order and came outside and asked Sukhi to come inside, saying they would stand in a corner. Sukhi agreed and went inside. Suddenly, Priya came towards them.

Sukhi was shocked to see her coming their way and turned around and went to the washroom. She told Mike that his order would be delayed for a while. Mike smiled and told her not to worry, he would wait. Priya smiled at him and left. Mike saw Sukhi's face as he was looking through the washroom window and laughed because his face went red after he saw that Priya was coming towards them. When Sukhi came back from the washroom, Mike told him that even he had been shocked to see her coming their way. Sukhi was still in shock.

While they were waiting for their food, Mike went into shock as this time he saw Courtney coming to the same McDonalds. She saw them and walked towards them. Mike saw her and immediately stopped talking, but Sukhi didn't know that Courtney was coming towards them. He was asking Mike what happened when, all of sudden, Courtney said "Hi!" to both of them. Sukhi was shocked and worried when he saw Courtney.

Courtney poked Sukhi and asked him why he didn't call her after that night. Sukhi apologised and said he was busy, and that he would call her soon. Courtney raised her eyebrows and asked him to call her as soon as he got free. Mike saw that Sukhi was looking shattered, so he interrupted and asked Courtney how she was doing. She replied with smile that she was fine and she was there with some friends to get lunch.

Mike and Sukhi breathed a sigh of relief when a staff member yelled out their coupon number; Mike took his food and went outside. Sukhi told Courtney that he would text her soon and left. Mike was bit surprised at the way in which they had handled that awkward situation.

While they entered their workplace, Sukhi was a bit upset and didn't want to have his lunch, so he went straight to his cabin. Mike followed him and sat down next to him. After a long silence, Mike told Sukhi he had a question. Sukhi nodded, and Mike asked him why he was so upset at not being together with Priya. Sukhi wondered why he asked this as he (Mike) knew that Sukhi was in love.

Before Sukhi could reply, Mike asked him another question: What made Sukhi so sad – was it Priya not being with him, or his not being able to talk to her? Sukhi shook his head. He replied after a while that he was in love with her, but couldn't imagine himself standing next to her. That upset him. He wanted her to be in his life so badly, that he would do anything for her. Mike smiled and said that, then, Sukhi should approach her instead of cursing himself for her not accepting his friend request on Facebook.

Sukhi thought about it deeply and convinced himself that he should approach her physically, and not on some social networking site. So, when he finished at work, he drove to the McDonalds. He wanted to go inside and approach her, but he didn't have the courage to do so. So, he waited outside and watched her work. She was helping one of the staff and training another simultaneously. She looked tired, and wiped the sweat from her forehead time to time, but continued working. Sukhi admired her ability to help others and to work hard.

After sometime, Sukhi went to his apartment and lay down on the couch and watched the sports channel on TV. After a while, he made himself a drink and switched on his laptop. He opened up his Facebook to see if she had accepted her friend request. She hadn't accepted his request, which made him sad. He decided to cancel the friend request and send her some flowers without mentioning his name on the card – this would help him forget her.

He wanted to discuss this with Mike, so he called and told him the plan. Mike applauded his plan and said he could send the flowers – after that, Sukhi had to ask Courtney out, so that he could get over Priya. Sukhi appreciated his help and ordered a bouquet online from one of the best florists in Sydney.

The next morning, on the way to work, he went to the florist and mentioned special delivery terms for the flowers he had ordered last night – the delivery should be after lunch time, so that Priya would receive the flowers herself, and there should be no note attached to it with the information of sender. He paid for the flowers and went back to his car and drove to his work.

He stopped at McDonalds for coffee, to make sure Priya had come to work. While waiting for his coffee, he saw Priya working at the back, putting up some papers on the notice board. Sukhi realised he didn't want to forget her, but he had no other option. So he took his coffee and drove to his workplace.

He went to his cabin and start doing some work when Mike came and asked him about the flowers. Sukhi replied that he did order some flowers and it was going to be delivered to her after lunch. Mike then made a plan with him and said they would go to McDonalds after lunch to see her reaction when she got those flowers. But Sukhi refused, saying that he wanted to forget about her. A couple of hours later, Sukhi caught himself thinking about Priya, and wondering what she would think after getting those flowers.

While he was imagining all this, Mike came in and interrupted him and said that he had gone to McDonalds to get lunch, and he had seen Priya getting those flowers. She looked very surprised as she couldn't figure out who sent them to her. At first, she had jumped with happiness at receiving those beautiful flowers and then she asked the delivery guy who had sent them but the delivery person refused to say and then Priya's face fell.

She called someone after that, and went to her office at the back and didn't come back outside until Mike left.

Sukhi became tense as it meant that she was seriously committed to someone else, and that she thought that the other guy had sent her the flowers. Mike told him to cheer up, as Sukhi had already decided to move on. But Sukhi replied that he couldn't live without her, and that he was madly in love with her, and broke into tears.

Mike said that Sukhi should not think like that as he didn't know her properly, and that she might not be his type. Sukhi replied that he would try to avoid the topic from then on, and it would be great if Mike could come over to his place in the evening with his girlfriend Katherine. Mike said he would be there, but Sukhi had to call Courtney as well to divert his mind from Priya, and he had to spend some quality time with Courtney. Sukhi said he would call Courtney.

While Sukhi was driving to his apartment, he called Courtney and invited her to come over his place for dinner, then stopped at the grocery store on the way. He then went to a liquor store next door and bought some drinks.

While he was coming out of the store, he bumped into someone and dropped the bottles on the ground. The other person was a girl, who also dropped everything that she was holding. When Sukhi saw her face, he was shocked to see that he had bumped into Priya. While she was busy picking her stuff, Priya was swearing at that guy whom she bumped into – but she didn't know who it was.

Suddenly, she stopped picking up her stuff and looked at him; he began helping her as he already picked up his things. Priya was busy staring at Sukhi so she forgot her stuff. They looked into each other's eyes and smiled. She even forgot that she was mad at him as it was his fault and completely forgotten about that incident after looking into his eyes.

When they both got up, Sukhi handed over her stuff. She apologised for her silly behaviour and said it was her fault, but Sukhi also apologised saying that he should have looked straight while walking instead of looking into his phone. They both smiled and walked in opposite directions, but kept looking back at each other and smiling.

When Sukhi went to his car, he again looked back but couldn't find her. From the other side of the road, Priya was watching him looking for her. She hoped that he would look at her standing on the other side of the road, but Sukhi didn't see her and then he got into his car and drove away.

While Sukhi was driving to his apartment, he thought about that incident over and over again. He completely forgot that he was expecting guests, and spent hours sitting in the balcony. Mike and Katherine arrived and knocked on the door. Sukhi was surprised at first, and then he remembered that he had invited them.

Sukhi apologised to Mike and said he had completely forgotten about them. Mike was surprised since Sukhi was the one who invited them to his place. Sukhi then told them to come inside and said that he would be ready in a minute.

When he came back, he said he would cook some food and went to kitchen. Katherine accompanied him to the kitchen, while Mike was busy playing some games on the Play Station.

While Sukhi and Katherine prepared the food, Mike came over and asked where Courtney was. Sukhi realised that he had to pick her up from her apartment, when interestingly at the same time, the door bell rang. Mike and Sukhi pleaded with Katherine to open the door as Courtney would kill Sukhi if she saw him. Katherine smiled and opened the door.

Courtney was very angry at the door and she went furious when she saw Katherine opening the door. She asked Katherine about where Sukhi was and then she told Katherine that Sukhi had ditched her – he was supposed to pick her up from her apartment, but he had forgotten and she had to get there by taxi.

Sukhi was hiding behind Mike. He apologised to Courtney, and Mike shouted that he had forgotten about them as well. Courtney and Katherine laughed at the way Mike shouted. Courtney hugged Sukhi and then they all settled down to have some drinks.

Katherine and Courtney were in the kitchen, while Sukhi and Mike were in the balcony having a drink. Mike then asked Sukhi about the reason behind his negligence, as he usually never forgot his commitments. Sukhi almost spat out his drink, with that question and he was also surprised that Mike knew that something was amiss.

Sukhi asked Mike why he thought that something was wrong. Mike then looked in his eyes and said he had known Sukhi for so long, and that he had seen his every expression. He again asked Sukhi about his negligence, and Sukhi told him everything that happened outside the grocery store. Mike was surprised at Priya's reaction outside the store, but he suggested that Sukhi forget about Priya as Courtney was also a nice girl. Sukhi replied that he was in two minds, and he needed some more time to think about things. He would let fate decide about his love life. He added that he needed Priya in his life and he would beg fate for her.

Dinner was served on the dining table, and the girls called them both to go inside. While they were eating, Sukhi and Mike were very quiet. Katherine asked Mike how the food was. Mike said it was fine, and she asked Sukhi the same question. Sukhi also said it was totally fine. He added that he liked it when someone else cooked food for him in his kitchen. Everyone laughed at his comment.

After they finished their dinner, everyone sat on the couch and watched a movie. Courtney had bought dessert for them – it was a chocolate cake that she had made. Everyone loved the cake, especially Sukhi. When she saw Sukhi looking happy, Courtney was delighted. She also liked his way of saying that he loved the cake with a smile and wink.

When everybody was getting ready to leave, Mike whispered to Sukhi to ask Courtney to stay a little longer. Courtney heard that and smiled at Sukhi, but Sukhi looked angrily at Mike. Katherine and Mike left; Courtney shut the door and came back to Sukhi.

They both sat on the couch and started watching the same movie. After some time, Sukhi said he was tired and wanted to go to bed, but Courtney wanted to ask him some questions. She asked him whether he liked her or not. Sukhi paused for a bit and then said he liked her, but he liked her as a friend and not more than that. Courtney said that she was not after his money or anything, like every other girl.

She liked him as more than a friend and wanted to be with him. Sukhi said he needed some more time to get over someone, and he couldn't even talk about that right now. Courtney was angry and said he had to tell her right away, but Sukhi refused to say a single word, which made her angry. She then stood up and said she would get going if Sukhi was not even interested in her. Sukhi asked her if he could drop her home, but she refused and left.

After that incident, a couple of days passed. One morning, Sukhi was not feeling well and had decided to take a day off from work. He also wanted to have some time off from his schedule to think about his personal life. He called up his office and told them he wouldn't be able to get in to work. He had some pills for his headache, and decided to get some video games as he had nothing new to play with. After sometime, Mike called him and asked him the reason for not coming in to office. Sukhi said he had had a headache; he was feeling better now but wanted some time off to figure things out. Mike then told him that he would come over after work and they could go for a movie if he had no plans. Sukhi replied that he had nothing planned as yet and he would be able to come for a movie.

At the gaming store, Sukhi was busy looking into the new release section of that store, when from the side of his vision; he saw that Priya was also at the same store. He wondered why she was coming in his way, now when he wanted to go away from her. Where was she hiding all those times when he was running after her?

Sukhi went to another aisle to browse some games and found himself in the same aisle as Priya. At one time, they crossed each other way and Priya saw Sukhi and smiled at him; Sukhi smiled back but he didn't talk to her, so she walked away. When Priya walked away, Sukhi felt very bad – he was sure that she was not interested in him and he had made the right decision to get over her. He took the games that he wanted and went to the counter to pay.

When Sukhi got back to his apartment, he was still unsure about Priya's behaviour so he called Mike and told him about seeing Priya. Mike got irritated and yelled at him to get over her and call Courtney. "Why don't you tell Courtney that you want to be with her and stay happy and blessed?" said Mike. Sukhi told him to calm down and said he would do the same and hung up the phone.

Sukhi then called up Courtney without knowing that she was still angry at him from the last incident at his place. Courtney picked up his call and rudely asked what he wanted now. Sukhi was shocked to hear her rude response so he politely asked her once again. Courtney yelled at him and said she was still angry with him as he had never called back to apologise. Sukhi then asked her what he had to apologise for. This made Courtney even angrier, as he had forgotten all about incident at his place, but she somehow explained it to him. He apologised for the incident and for forgetting about that night as well. He said he had called to ask if she would go with him to a movie that night. Moreover, he had called in sick – if she was free, she could join him for lunch, and they could be together in the evening as well. Courtney instantly forgot her anger and shouted with joy, and said she would love to join him but he had to pick her up from her apartment.

After some time, Sukhi went to pick up Courtney from her apartment. Courtney opened the door. She was very well dressed and Sukhi praised her choice of clothes, which made her blush. They both went down to his car. When they both sat in the car, Sukhi asked Courtney where she wanted to go for lunch and started the car. Courtney said she wanted to try Indian food; Sukhi smiled and drove to an Indian restaurant with her.

When they reached the parking lot of the restaurant, Sukhi came over and opened the car door for Courtney, which she appreciated very much. When they entered the Indian restaurant, everyone stared at them as though they had seen an alien coming out from a spaceship. Sukhi whispered in Courtney's ear that this was the reason he always avoided going to Indian restaurants with his friends. Courtney told him to ignore them.

Sukhi asked the concierge for a table for two, and said it would be best if the table was next to a window and not near the kitchen. The concierge showed them to a table and they sat down. Sukhi even pulled out the chair for Courtney to sit down first; she was overwhelmed by his gesture and blushed.

Sukhi offered her the menu and asked her to order. Courtney said she had never tried Indian food before, so he could order for her as well. She just didn't want spicy or oily food. Sukhi ordered some mild curries and rice for Courtney, and he ordered his favourite South Indian dish, dosa, for himself.

While they were waiting for the food, Sukhi and Courtney talked about their love for nature and planned to go to a lake after lunch. Sukhi said they could wait there till the sun set, as it would be a lovely sight.

After lunch, they headed towards the lake. Courtney was feeling very happy in Sukhi's company, and Sukhi was also enjoying the time with her. They walked along the side of the lake and enjoyed the nice breeze. Courtney was feeling a bit cold, so Sukhi handed over his blazer and said she could have it. Courtney put it on and put her arm under his shoulder and leaned on his shoulder. They walked slowly until they reached the last bench on the path. Courtney sat on the bench and asked Sukhi to come over.

Sukhi slowly went there and stood behind that bench. Courtney turned and looked at Sukhi and asked him the same question – whether he liked her or not. Sukhi walked over to sit next to her. He said she was a very nice girl and he would like to spend time with her, but he didn't want to hurt her feelings and that he needed some more time to make up his mind. Courtney said she was in no rush, and that he could take his time. She also thanked him for a beautiful evening.

They were enjoying the sunset at the lake. Courtney said she had come to this lake many times, but today it looked like heaven. Sukhi suddenly got a call from Mike – they had planned to watch a movie earlier, but Sukhi had completely forgotten about. Mike was yelling at him over the phone as he had been waiting for Sukhi to call. Sukhi apologised and said that they would be there shortly and Mike can go ahead and buy the tickets.

Sukhi and Courtney drove to the theatre and saw Mike and Keth standing outside, waiting for them. Sukhi asked Mike if he had bought the tickets; Mike said he had. Sukhi said he would buy popcorn and some drinks. On his way back, he again bumped into a girl – Priya!

Priya smiled at him. Sukhi dropped the food on the floor and made a mess. They were busy looking at each other when Mike came to rescue him. Courtney and Keth were standing far away, but Mike knew that it was going to be hard for Sukhi to forget Priya if they kept bumping into each other.

Mike told Sukhi that he would grab the drinks, and Sukhi could go to the bathroom and dry himself, as the drink had spilt on his arms. Sukhi went to the bathroom and Priya went back to her friends.

When they entered the theatre, Courtney and Keth sat in between Sukhi and Mike. Unexpectedly, Priya came in and sat down next to Sukhi. She smiled at Sukhi again. They were watching the movie when, all of a sudden, Priya's hand touched Sukhi's hand. They both looked at each other and completely forgot about the movie. They didn't know what was going on with them, as they came there with someone else but now wanted to talk to each other.

Courtney saw that and nudged Sukhi to see the movie and not Priya's face. Priya noticed that, and she felt uncomfortable, so she changed seats with her friend who was sitting next to her. Sukhi was disappointed, and became angry with Courtney.

When the movie finished, they came outside. Sukhi was already standing outside as he was feeling uncomfortable in the hall and he had come outside for the fresh air. Mike went to Sukhi and asked him why he had left. Mike also added that it was rude and that Courtney was crying inside after Sukhi left. Sukhi told Mike about what had happened in the theatre, and that he didn't want Courtney to know that he was looking at that girl whom he had feelings for; and also that he was more attracted to Priya than Courtney, but he didn't want to break Courtney's heart. Mike talked to Courtney and calmed her down, and told Sukhi to drop her to her apartment.

While Sukhi was driving, he asked Courtney whether she had liked the movie. Courtney didn't reply. Sukhi then changed the question and asked if she had liked the popcorn. Courtney smiled a bit, but turned her face away from Sukhi and looked out of the window. Sukhi asked her if she had liked the Pepsi. Courtney then smiled and said, "You don't even know how to make a girl happy". Sukhi asked her why she was angry with him at the first place. Courtney looked at Sukhi angrily, and Sukhi knew that she was about to ask him a lot of questions, but he asked her again why she was angry. Courtney asked loudly, "Who was she?"

"Who was who?" asked Sukhi. "That girl at the theatre to whom you were staring". Courtney yelled at him. "I don't know her," Sukhi said, but she didn't believe him and told him not to call her again. Sukhi quietly drove her to her apartment.

Next morning, when he went to work, Sukhi went to Mike's cabin and told him that Courtney had told him not to call her. Mike looked surprised, and said, "You wanted that, isn't it?" Sukhi was shocked and said he didn't want to hurt Courtney; she seemed to be a nice girl and he didn't know what she was thinking about him. Mike immediately said "bad things" and laughed. Mike then asked Sukhi to try calling her and it would be alright. Sukhi agreed and said he would give it a try after work.

When he finished work, Sukhi stopped by at McDonalds again and looked for Priya. This time, Priya also looked at Sukhi – which made Sukhi feel tense, so he walked off from the car park. While driving back to his apartment, he was thinking that if he hadn't seen her in the supermarket he would have had a better chance of asking her out for a coffee. When he reached his apartment, he picked up his laptop and went to Priya's profile on Facebook and looked at her pictures. He then cooked his dinner and completely forgot about calling Courtney.

Some days passed, and Sukhi became very busy at work, and he completely forgot about Priya and Courtney. Also, his family, who was in America, planned to visit him but couldn't make it, Sukhi, was a bit upset as he hadn't met his family for the past six years, and he wanted to be with them.

One morning, when he went to work, he went straight to his cabin and started doing his work. After some time, someone knocked on his cabin door. It was Courtney. Sukhi was shocked to see Courtney there, and he was surprised that she had come inside without a visitors pass. Courtney sat on the chair as Mike walked in. Mike asked Sukhi to apologise to Courtney; she had been crying for two days as he hadn't called her. Sukhi apologised but told her to go before their boss saw her; if someone saw her, Mike and he would get into trouble. He promised to call her in the evening and visit her apartment after work. Courtney was happy with that response and thanked Mike for arranging the meeting.

Sukhi was angry with Mike for doing all this without asking him.

At lunch time, Mike came to Sukhi's cabin. Sukhi refused to go to lunch with him, and said he wouldn't have lunch with a friend who betrayed him. Mike smiled and said, "You will miss me". Sukhi shook his head and said he would die before missing him. Mike pleaded with him to forgive his action – he had no other way of fixing it as she kept calling him and Keth and crying on the phone. Sukhi asked Mike why he was trying so hard to hook him up with Courtney.

Mike then told him that he just wanted Sukhi to be happy. After Priya came into his life, Sukhi had completely changed into a different person. Mike missed the old Sukhi, who always laughed and cracked jokes and threw parties all the time. Sukhi said he was still the same, but he was bit confused. He loved Priya but he was not sure if she felt the same or not. Mike then told him to forget about Priya – it was just an attraction and nothing else. He assured Sukhi that he would find him a girl who was nicer than Priya. In the meantime, he could go out with Courtney to get over Priya.

Sukhi said he would think about it, but he didn't want to hurt Courtney as well. She had some feelings for him and he didn't want to get involved in that situation as he only viewed her as a friend. Mike told him to at least give it a try since she was nice girl; he also thought that Courtney did love him, and that's why he was trying hard to get them together. Sukhi nodded and said, "Let's have lunch now", and that he would stop by at Courtney's place after work.

After work, Sukhi went to Courtney's place. Courtney opened the door and saw Sukhi standing outside with a wine bottle in his hand. She was in her pyjamas. Sukhi gave her the wine and asked her, "What's for dinner?" Courtney asked what he would like. Sukhi replied with a smile, "Indian food". She smiled and said he could go and freshen up, and she would order some food from the Indian restaurant where they had had lunch other day.

Courtney called up the restaurant and ordered some Indian curries and naans. Sukhi came back from the restroom and sat down next to Courtney. Courtney cuddled up to him and said romantically that she would love to live with him. Sukhi got upset, and stood up. He said he would not visit her again if she said anything about marriage as he hadn't thought so far yet. Courtney said it was alright, and she wouldn't ask him again until he felt like proposing to her. They both agreed on that.

Suddenly, somebody knocked on the door. Courtney thought her food delivery had come, but when she opened the door it was Mike and Keth standing with a bag of food and beer. Courtney was shocked and said, "Guys, why didn't you tell me? I could have worn something nicer than pyjamas." Mike told Courtney he didn't mind her in pyjamas but Keth gave him an angry look. Mike then smiled and said he was just joking.

When they entered the apartment, Sukhi was on the couch, watching sports on the TV. Mike then told him to switch off the TV and have drinks with them. Sukhi said he didn't feel like drinking but asked them what was for dinner as he was hungry. Mike said it was Chinese. Sukhi said he didn't feel like eating Chinese at moment. Mike then asked him to order some other food for himself. Courtney told Mike that she had already ordered some Indian food for them.

Mike told Courtney, "You are getting ready to be an Indian bride!" Sukhi looked at him angrily, so Mike then zipped his lips and said he wouldn't say anything like that in future. Courtney smiled and said she would love to learn how to cook Indian food. Sukhi shouted at them to change the topic, and they all agreed.

While they were waiting for the food to arrive, Mike sat down next to Sukhi with a drink and handed over his drink, while Katherine and Courtney were in the kitchen heating up something to go with their dinner. Mike told Sukhi that he was confused about something and he really wanted his advice on it.

Sukhi said that apart from getting married to Courtney, he could ask him anything. Mike said that he was about to ask him about marriage but not of Sukhi or Courtney; he was thinking of proposing to Katherine. Sukhi got excited and asked if he had already proposed or not.

Mike said he hadn't proposed yet, but he wanted to propose soon and he wanted to know if he was doing the right thing or not. Sukhi assured him that he was about to make the best decision of his life and asked him to go for it. Mike said that Sukhi would be the best man at his wedding. Sukhi jumped up with happiness and said Mike should propose quickly then as he would love to be the best man at his wedding.

While they were talking, someone knocked on the door – it was the delivery guy for the food that Courtney had ordered. Sukhi went to pay but Mike refused to let him, and paid for the food. They finished their drinks and headed over to the dining table.

The four of them had a nice dinner. When everyone was getting ready to leave, Courtney asked Sukhi to stay for a bit but he said he had to go to finish up some accounts, and that he would visit her the next day. Courtney smiled and said, "Fine".

While Sukhi was driving home, he saw Priya accompanied by the same guy, walking outside the Indian restaurant where he had gone with Courtney. Priya seemed very happy, and was smiling and talking to the guy. Sukhi assumed that she was happy with someone else and that he had to move on in his life.

After some days, when Sukhi was at work, Mike came to Sukhi's cabin and gave him surprising news – Keth was pregnant and they were expecting a baby! Sukhi congratulated him and called Keth on her cell phone to congratulate her as well. They were very happy and Sukhi invited them to his apartment, and called Courtney as well. Mike was jumping with happiness. Sukhi hugged Mike and said he was really happy for him.

Sukhi then again asked Mike if he had proposed to Keth for marriage or not. Mike said he wanted to, but now was not the right time.

While Sukhi was going to his apartment, he stopped by at the florist to get a nice bouquet for Keth and Mike. He was browsing through the store and saw a beautiful bouquet of mixed flowers, but the sales person told him that it was already been sold to another customer. The sales person then pointed to Priya. Sukhi saw Priya and instantly turned his face away and start looking for some other flowers.

While Priya was browsing the store for some other flowers, she looked at Sukhi and smiled, to which Sukhi also responded with smile and then looked for a corner to hide from her. After couple of minutes, Sukhi chose a bouquet and bought it and went outside. His eyes were looking for Priya but couldn't find her.

When he got into his car, he saw Priya walking along the street. He stopped his car on the side where she was walking and asked her if she needed a ride home. She said she was fine, but Sukhi said he didn't have any problem dropping her home.

She got into his car and told him to drop her next block. Sukhi's heartbeat was very strong and loud at that time. It could be heard by anyone – boom boom.

Sukhi wanted to start a conversation, so he gathered his guts and said, "My name is Sukhi". She replied with a smile, "Nice to meet you Sukhi. My name is Priya". They both smiled at each other.

There was an awkward silence for a while. Priya was not looking at him but she wanted to start a conversation with him, as she secretly liked him. After a couple of seconds, she asked, "Oh, this is for your girlfriend?"

Sukhi smiled and replied, "No, it's for my friends Mike and Keth – they are expecting their first baby." Priya then said, "Nice choice". "Really" Sukhi asked excitedly and smiled.

Sukhi was about to say something when she said "Drop me here. My apartment is in that building." Sukhi stopped the car in front of the building, but she got out of the car very slowly as thought she wanted to stay there.

Sukhi said it was nice meeting her, and she replied she felt the same, and then went inside the building. Sukhi was watching her for a while, then he saw his watch and realised he was getting late. Mike and Keth would be waiting outside his apartment.

Sukhi went to the liquor store and bought some drinks, and ordered for pizza to be delivered at his apartment. When he reached his apartment, Mike and Keth were waiting outside his apartment. Sukhi apologised and hugged them both and congratulated them.

He gave Keth the bouquet and said he was very happy for them. Mike then asked where Courtney was – Sukhi had again forgotten to pick her up. Sukhi then gave his apartment keys to them, and said he would go and pick Courtney up.

Sukhi then went to Courtney's house and knocked on the door. Courtney replied rudely that if it was Sukhi, she wouldn't open the door as he was late. Sukhi pleaded for forgiveness and said he was busy finding a nice bouquet for Keth and Mike. She asked him why he was buying them flowers. He said it was a surprise as they were expecting a baby. That's why he was late.

Courtney then opened the door. She was wearing a nice black dress and Sukhi couldn't stop himself from saying she looked very pretty. Courtney smiled and said, "Thanks. Let's go".

When they reached Sukhi's apartment, they saw that Mike and Keth were kissing each other. Sukhi intentionally coughed and entered the apartment. Courtney hugged Keth and congratulated her. There was loud music playing in Sukhi's apartment, and then they all danced to the beat. After some time, Mike and Sukhi went to the balcony and Mike asked him in a strange tone about the reason for today's negligence? Sukhi smiled and told him about dropping Priya to her apartment.

Mike couldn't believe it, so Sukhi said he was not lying. Mike said there was a little hope, but Sukhi refused and said she had talked to him only because she needed a ride home. Just then, Courtney interrupted them and said food was ready, but Sukhi told her to wait for a while.

Somebody knocked the door of the apartment. Sukhi told Mike to open the door – when he opened it, there was a guy standing there with a two-tier cake in his hand. Mike was overwhelmed with the surprise and took the cake inside. Keth was also very happy and thanked Sukhi for the beautiful surprise.

Courtney hugged Sukhi tightly and whispered in his ear that it was really a very nice surprise, and that he was a very nice guy for planning it for them. She then kissed him on his cheek. Mike and Keth also ran towards Sukhi and hugged him. They spent whole evening planning a big party for a baby shower.

For a couple of weeks, Sukhi's life was going on smoothly. Priya kept coming and going in his life, but Sukhi didn't approach her as he always saw her with someone else. She hung around with the same guy all the time, so Sukhi convinced himself to stay away from her. But fate was not in Sukhi's favour.

One day, he saw Priya sitting on a bench next to the lake where he usually went for a walk. Priya was sitting alone, and she was crying. Before Sukhi could go and ask her if she needed any help, the same guy came up and tried to comfort her but she was not getting any better. It seemed like they were having some kind of argument.

Sukhi was standing behind a tree there and looking at them. He wanted to help her. After some time, the scene changed and the verbal arguments became more aggressive and they began to scream at each other. Priya was screaming at the guy to leave her alone; the guy said some inappropriate words to her and went away.

After the guy left, she started crying and Sukhi went over and sat next to Priya and said, "Hi". She didn't reply, and continued to cry and wipe her eyes. Sukhi handed over his hanky to wipe the tears. Then, he passed her his water bottle and sat there quietly. After some time, she calmed down. Sukhi was still sitting next to her quietly.

Sukhi asked her what had happened. She didn't reply, just sat there quietly. After a couple of minutes, she muttered, "Why is life so hard to live?" Sukhi smiled at that question, and said, "It's life – nobody has control over it. You just have to let it go sometimes. That will make you happy. Don't expect anything from anyone. Just live your life freely."

Priya looked up at him and smiled and said those were really very nice words. Sukhi again asked her what had happened and why she was crying. Priya said it was nothing, and she was going to let it go now. She got up and asked Sukhi if he could walk her home. Sukhi got up and started walking with her.

While they were walking towards Priya's house, Sukhi said he wanted to ask her something. Priya looked at him innocently and smiled and said, "Yeah sure". Sukhi asked her who the guy was with whom she was arguing. Priya said he was nothing to her anymore. Sukhi insisted that she could tell him more about that guy.

Priya told him that his name was Ronny, and he had been chosen by her elder brother for her to marry. She didn't like him as he was a male chauvinist; for him, girls were only meant to cook and feed. Sukhi was shocked and asked why she was still with him. "Why don't you tell your brother about him?" he asked.

Priya replied it didn't matter to her brother as Ronny was his wife's brother, and the wife was very cunning.

She (Priya's brother's wife) didn't like Priya's parents; her brother ruled her family, and nobody could say anything against him. She had come to Australia to get away from that bad environment.

Yet, fate was not on her side. Her brother chose a guy for her, and she couldn't oppose it because of her family also insisted on it. Her mother called her and asked her to give it a try because she (Priya's mother) was also afraid of her brother. If she refused, a big fight would take place back home, and she wouldn't be able to get in touch with her parents after that. That was the only reason she had said "Yes" to this guy. But now it became huge trouble for her as she couldn't go out with anyone, and couldn't have any friends coming over to her place. She also had to work two jobs to fulfil his desires, as he drank daily and gambled a lot.

While they were walking, Sukhi stopped for a bit and held her hand and said if that he could help her somehow, he would love to do that for her. Priya looked at him and asked him why he wanted to help her. Sukhi froze as he didn't have the courage to tell her about his true feelings for her – that he was in love with her and, for the sake of his love, he wanted to help her.

They looked at each other for a while, then Priya shook her head and said Sukhi should leave. If Ronny saw him walking with her, he would be angry and might try to hurt Sukhi.

Sukhi then asked her why she was so afraid for him. Priya stopped walking and looked into his eyes, but couldn't say anything. After a couple of seconds, she started walking towards her apartment. She didn't look back but walked very slowly, as if she wanted to go back and run away with Sukhi. Finally, she went inside the building.

Sukhi stood there for hours and wanted her to come back so that he could hug her and tell her how much he loved her. He waited for her the whole evening, and, later that evening, Sukhi fell completely in love with her.

Finally, he took a cab to go home. On the way home, he wondered about why she had shared those things with him. Now, he desperately wanted to help her out. This was the second time he fallen for her – this time, it was love for sure and he didn't want to let her go. He wanted to be with her forever.

On the other hand, Priya was also beginning to like Sukhi but she was not able to tell him so because of Ronny and her family. She remembered Sukhi had asked her why she was afraid for him; it was obvious that she didn't want anyone to hurt him. She completely forgotten about Ronny as he didn't exist for her and she was lying on the bed and dreaming about Sukhi and wanted to meet him again.

Next morning, when Sukhi met Mike at work, he told him everything about Priya and her issues with her family and Ronny. Mike was a bit upset about this, and asked, "Why does her brother have to choose a guy for her? Why can't she choose someone herself?"

Sukhi laughed at that question and said that in India, girls don't usually choose husbands for themselves – it's a tradition coming along from ancient times. India has developed a lot as a modern country, but Indians had not developed yet. That's why Sukhi had chosen to live in Australia – because he didn't want to live in a congested society where girls had no rights.

In some places, girls were not allowed to even show their faces to anyone except their family members and husbands. And if a girl chose to wear jeans and skirts, they were considered as sluts and whores. Mike was very shocked to hear all that. He told Sukhi and they would help Priya and free her from these restrictions.

Mike and Sukhi talked about Priya for the whole day, and they both wanted to help her but didn't know how. When they finished work, Sukhi insisted that Mike come to his apartment and spend some time with him, as he was feeling sad about Priya. Mike said that Sukhi was totally in love with Priya, but Sukhi just said he couldn't see anyone in tears and, from his bottom of heart, he wanted to help her.

When Sukhi finished work, he went to McDonalds and looked for Priya but couldn't find her. While he was leaving, someone called his name from inside – when he turned, he saw Priya calling him from inside. He went inside and saw that Priya had a black mark under her left eye. Priya told Sukhi not to come to McDonalds and not to follow her.

She was scared for him because Ronny had seen them together. When Sukhi insisted that she come outside for a bit, she refused. Sukhi then told her that he wouldn't leave until she came outside. He then went outside and stood next to his car.

After half an hour, Priya came outside and went towards Sukhi. Sukhi asked her what had happened under her eye. Priya said there was nothing wrong, and he had nothing to worry about. Sukhi angrily asked her what had happened. Priya then broke into tears and said Ronny had hit her last night because he had seen her with Sukhi.

She explained that when she had gone back to her apartment, she went to her bedroom. Ronny was in the balcony and he had seen Sukhi standing alone under that building; he also seen Sukhi walking with Priya. He went into the bedroom and slapped her; threw his drink on her and told her to cook dinner for him.

Sukhi lost his temper and said he would give Ronny a hard time, but Priya held his hand and asked him not to do anything – if not, she would get into more trouble. Sukhi said he would give Ronny something back in return, as he had done something terribly wrong with her. Priya begged Sukhi to promise her that he wouldn't do anything to Ronny. It was her life and Sukhi had nothing to do with it. Sukhi yelled, "Its fine!" but asked why she didn't tell her parents about this incident.

Priya said she had thought about that, but when she called her brother, the first thing he had asked was, "Who was that guy with you?" She had hung up the phone as she knew that Ronny had already told her brother about that incident. Sukhi was furious and said he would kill Ronny.

Priya then folded her hands and told him not to do anything; she begged him and tried to calm him down. Then she asked him if he could come to the same park on Sunday evening. Ronny was going to Melbourne on Sunday, and she could sneak out on that day. But she asked him to promise her that he wouldn't do anything before that.

Sukhi said he would be there, but she had to promise that she wouldn't cry after that day. He would do anything for her; he could even die for her. They hugged each other, then Priya told Sukhi to leave as her shift was about to finish and Ronny could come any time to pick her up.

When Mike went to Sukhi's apartment, Sukhi told him about how Ronny had treated Priya. Mike was shocked and said that Ronny was a coward. Mike then asked Sukhi about what he planned to do. Sukhi said he was going to meet Priya at the lake on Sunday – he would plan after that, because he was not sure if Priya would stand by him or not.

The next day, he stopped by at McDonalds. He saw Priya working at the drive-through window. She saw him at the carpark, but looked sad; Sukhi signalled to her that she had to smile. When Priya smiled at him, he waved and then drove to his workplace. At lunch time, Priya was thinking about Sukhi; he seemed like a nice guy who wanted everyone around him to smile.

She had developed feelings for Sukhi. That was the first time she felt something for a boy, and she started falling for him. She began to think about Sukhi all the time. While she was working or buying groceries or walking alone, Priya missed him and wanted him to be around her always, so she started imagining him as walking next to her.

On the other hand, Sukhi was happy as she had smiled at him, and it seemed as if she had some feelings for him too. Later that day, he was thinking about those days when he was running after her and when he sent her bouquet –he didn't find her after that day for so long, and he assumed that it might be because of Ronny.

When Sukhi finished work, he went to the McDonalds carpark and stood there for 20 minutes. Priya came outside to see him; she stood next to him but they didn't exchange any words for about 10 minutes. Sukhi asked her how she was doing; Priya nodded and asked him about his day.

Sukhi said he needed to tell her something. Priya thought he was going to propose to her, which was not a good idea. Still, she told him to say whatever it was. Sukhi said that the flowers that she had received the other day were sent by him. Priya gave him a surprised look and said that it had been was a nice idea to send the flowers, but that she had gotten into trouble for those. Sukhi asked her why she had gotten into trouble.

Priya told him that she didn't know who had sent those flowers as there was no note attached to it – and she thought they were sent by Ronny. But when she got home and thanked Ronny for the flowers, he got angry and told her that he didn't send them. He slapped her, and she slipped and knocked her knee against the kitchen table. Her knee was badly hurt and she couldn't go to work for two weeks.

Sukhi apologised and said he didn't know those flowers would land her in trouble. Priya told him to not to worry – it was not his fault as, at that time, he didn't know anything about Ronny and her life. Sukhi said he was very angry that Ronny was a coward who had no guts to fight against boys. Priya also thought the same, but she couldn't do anything as her family would be in trouble. Sukhi assured her that he would think of something to get her out of that situation – but she had to trust him. Priya assured him that she trusted him as he was a nice person. Sukhi smiled and gave her a hug.

All of a sudden, Priya told him to leave as she was about to finish her shift and Ronny would be there soon. Sukhi said he was not afraid, and he had the guts to stand in front of anybody, but Priya insisted that he'd better leave as she didn't want any trouble. They exchanged phone numbers, and Sukhi told her to be strong. He added that she was the most beautiful girl he had ever seen in his life.

Priya smiled and hugged him tight and said, "Please go now, as Ronny will be here soon". Sukhi chuckled and said she had to let go so that he could go. They smiled and went their own way.

When Sukhi was cooking dinner at home, his phone beeped. It was Priya's text message saying that there was no trouble today – hurray – and a smiley face at the end. Sukhi replied by saying that was nice and put a smiley face at the end.

She replied and asked him what he was doing. Sukhi said he was cooking himself dinner and put a sad smiley face.

She asked him what he was cooking. Sukhi said that he was making scrambled eggs as he had forgotten to buy groceries. Priya asked him why he forgot and added a laughing smiley. Sukhi held his phone for a minute and replied that it slipped from his mind as he was busy thinking of someone else. Priya understood his words and sent a blushing smiley and asked him who was on his mind. When Sukhi saw the message he forgot that he was cooking and his scrambled eggs were burnt. He replied that she knew better who was in his mind.

Priya smiled at that message and blushed. She texted him back and asked if it was someone she knew. Sukhi was smiling and blushing, and in full audacity sent her a message: "It's you". She didn't reply after that. Sukhi was feeling anxious, and he suddenly realised that his eggs were burnt and he had nothing else to eat.

He was still thinking of her and wondering why she didn't reply. Then, after an hour, she replied "Oh really". Sukhi was relieved and was ready to pick up something from a takeaway nearby. While driving to the takeaway, he sent Priya another message asking what took her so long to reply.

He reached the takeaway and ordered a burger and some chips and, while waiting, he received another message from her saying that Ronny had come into her room and she had pretended to be asleep. Sukhi said he was worried for her; he thought she might get into trouble for texting him. He said that he was now at the takeaway to get something to eat as his scrambled eggs were burnt.

Priya replied with a sad smiley and a hug smiley. Sukhi replied with the same smiley and picked up his food and went back to his car. She replied that she was a bit tired and Ronny kept coming to her room. She sent a kiss smiley and said good night. Sukhi wished her good night and sweet dreams and told her to take care.

Next day when he woke up, saw a text message from Priya with a 'Good Morning' and a smiley. While going for work, he stopped at McDonalds and ordered his coffee. He saw Priya working at the back; she seemed busy, so he didn't disturb her. He took his coffee and went to work.

While he was in his cabin, Mike came in and asked him what happened – he had been standing outside, but Sukhi had ignored him and gone to his cabin. Sukhi was surprised and said "Sorry, Mike". Mike laughed at him and said he was joking as he had come in late. Sukhi then told him to leave as he had some work to do. Mike then smiled and said he would be back by lunchtime to annoy him.

Sukhi got busy at work, when all of sudden his phone beeped – it was Priya's text message saying that she was going to be free at lunchtime and she would give him company if he was willing to have lunch with her. Sukhi replied that he was free and he would pick her up around lunchtime, and then they could go somewhere to have lunch together. He asked her if she had any particular preference on where she wanted to go.

Priya replied that he could take her anywhere he liked. Sukhi jumped with joy and said they could go to a Mexican restaurant next to his workplace. She said 'yes' with a smiley face. Sukhi was overwhelmed at that response and had a strong vibe that she also liked him the way he liked her. Sukhi then rushed to Mike's cabin and said he was going for lunch with Priya at the Mexican restaurant. Mike jumped up with joy, and said that she was finally getting out from her comfort zone, which was fantastic. Mike hugged Sukhi and said he was happy to see him happy after so long.

At lunchtime, Sukhi went to McDonalds and picked up Priya, and they went to the Mexican restaurant. They went inside and sat at a corner table. Priya was smiling and Sukhi appreciated her effort. One of the waiters approached them and asked them what they wished to have. Sukhi gave the menu card to Priya and asked her to order for both of them. Priya said she didn't know much about Mexican food, and told him to order for her as well. So Sukhi ordered enchiladas for both of them, and asked if she wanted it spicy or mild. She said she didn't eat meat, so Sukhi had to order something vegetarian. Sukhi smiled and ordered vegetarian enchiladas for her and chicken enchiladas for him and some drinks to go with it.

While they were waiting for their food, Priya told Sukhi that she had been thinking about him all night. Sukhi smiled and said the same thing happened to him as well, as he was worried also for her and didn't want to see tears in her eyes. Priya looked down and blushed. Sukhi understood that she was also in love with him.

Sukhi's confidence shot up and he smiled at her. Priya looked like she wanted to say something to him but she didn't say anything. Sukhi observed that and asked her what she was about to say.

Priya refused to say anything and just looked down. Sukhi insisted that she had to say whatever it was. Priya smiled and said that she had some feelings for him. Sukhi was overwhelmed, and said he also shared the same feelings with her. Priya nodded and said she knew that. She added that she never felt that way for anyone else before. Sukhi replied with a smile. Just then, the waiter interrupted them and gave them their food.

Sukhi gave her the vegetarian enchiladas and said she would be happy to have Mexican food if she hadn't tried it before. Priya took a bite and said the food was nice. Sukhi asked that what she would do if Ronny saw them together having lunch. Priya said she didn't care about that as she liked Sukhi more than anyone. It was her life and nobody had any control over it except her. Sukhi was surprised at her confidence and said she had come a long way out from her comfort zone.

Priya replied that she had a person sitting in front of her who could give her all the happiness she desired. On the other side, she had one person who could give her trouble and make her life a living hell. So she chose to live with Sukhi rather than die every day with Ronny.

Sukhi promised her that she would never be sad in her life if she stood by him. Priya told him she was not sure, as she may not be able to take that much pain. Also, she didn't want Sukhi to get into trouble. Sukhi assured her that he wouldn't get into trouble. He also told her that he wouldn't let her go into that deep hole from which he wouldn't be able to pull her out. She had to think before she tied the knot with Ronny.

Priya went into deep thought, and quietly ate her food. Sukhi was also quiet as he knew that he had to be sure if she would stand by him or not. He was sure that if she would stand by him, he would never let her go after that, and no one could come in between them.

Priya finished her food and Sukhi went to the counter to pay. While Sukhi was paying, he saw that Priya was still in deep thought. He knew that she was going to be with him, but he wanted to make sure that she be true to her feelings for him. They both went out quietly. Sukhi dropped Priya at McDonalds and said he would see her after work. Priya sat there for a bit and then hugged him before getting out. Sukhi waited until she went inside and waved to him.

Sukhi then drove to his workplace, and saw Mike waiting for him in his cabin. Sukhi smiled and said he had had a nice lunch with Priya, and that Priya also liked him. Mike jumped up on his chair and start dancing on it with happiness. Sukhi shouted to him to come down, and added that she had told him that she liked him and she would be with him but she needed some more time to think as she didn't want him to get involved in trouble.

Mike said he was with them and there was nothing to worry about. Sukhi then told Mike that they had to go to India to get married. Mike told Sukhi to come out of his dream, as she hadn't yet told him that she would marry him. Sukhi just nodded and laughed.

When Sukhi finished work, he went to McDonalds and stood outside, leaning on his car. After 10 minutes, Priya came outside and stood next to him. Sukhi asked her how the day was going; she said it was nice and steady. Sukhi then asked what she thought about them. She said that she wanted to be with him, but that if someone hurt him she would never forgive herself. Sukhi held her hand and said there would be no trouble if she was with him. He could give up his life for her happiness and he needed her to trust him.

Priya smiled and said she would always be with him, and Sukhi had to promise her that he would never leave her alone. Sukhi promised that he would never leave her in any condition. He would always stand by her, and give her all the happiness of the world. Priya then said those three magical words to Sukhi: I LOVE YOU. Sukhi jumped with joy and said that this day was the most wonderful and special day in his life. He would never forget that day. Priya said she wanted him to make this day equally special for her as well.

Sukhi held Priya's hand and pulled her towards him and kissed her.

It was their first kiss ever, and a wonderful moment. They both felt so special, as if nobody existed around there and they didn't even need any attention as they felt like they were in the heaven and wanted to live there forever. Both of them closed their eyes and were enjoying each other's presence in their life. Priya was holding Sukhi's hands tightly, and Sukhi was gently rubbing his hand over her hair.

After the kiss, Priya blushed and thanked Sukhi for making her day so special. She would never forget that moment in her life – even after death. Sukhi said that she shouldn't say anything about death as they would live long, their love would keep growing day by day, and no one could separate them at any cost.

Next day, as planned, they were going to see each other at the lake. Sukhi had already planned a nice evening out with Priya. He went there first and sat on the last bench that was situated next to one end of the lake; no one would disturb them there. From that bench, the view was also unique as they could see the lake and a bit of the bushes. The sunset from that bench was fabulous.

Priya came to the lake, and Sukhi sent her a text message saying that he was on the last bench around the corner. Priya came and sat next to him. She was wearing a traditionally Punjabi suit with the tikka on her forehead. When Sukhi saw that, he couldn't stop himself from saying that she looked gorgeous in traditional clothes. She smiled when Sukhi praised her; she had never felt that before because Ronny never praised her.

Sukhi then started the conversation by asking that if Ronny had gone to Melbourne or not. Priya told him not to talk about Ronny. Sukhi smiled and asked her to tell him something more about herself. Priya said she was from a small town in Punjab, and that she had an elder sister who had gotten married last year and settled in the London, United Kingdom. Priya wanted to go there but had ended up in Australia.

Sukhi chuckled and said it was his good luck and kissed Priya's forehead. Priya was leaning on his chest; she took his arm and put it on her shoulder so that she could easily lie down there. Sukhi then asked her how she would manage all those obstacles to their being in love. Priya empathetically said she would kill everyone who came in between them. Sukhi laughed at her answer and said she couldn't even kill a mosquito, and now she wanted to kill everyone who would come in between them.

Priya then got up and said she was a strong girl who could fight with anyone. If he didn't believe her, he could try it. Sukhi broke into loud laughter and said he wouldn't even think of fighting with her. He couldn't stop laughing, and Priya also joined in the laughter.

After some time, Priya asked him about himself, but Sukhi said she hadn't finished her story. Priya asked him what else he wanted to know. Sukhi said he wanted to know what her future plans were. She said she wanted to study fashion designing, but, unfortunately, her family didn't support her so she ended up doing management, but she was enjoying it. Then Priya asked Sukhi to tell her about himself.

Sukhi said he was also from a small town from Punjab. His family was in America and he had an elder sister who was married and settled in Vancouver, Canada. He wanted to be an actor but ended up doing accountancy. Priya said he could be an actor as he was smart and attractive, but Sukhi said he had no dream of being an actor now.

They spent the whole evening there and enjoyed a nice sunset by the lake. Priya asked where they were going to go. Sukhi said he would take her to a nice Indian restaurant if she was willing to go out with him. Priya said she had no problem going there, but it was not a good idea as they might know someone there and Ronny might find out about them. Sukhi said she still hadn't come out of her comfort zone; Priya looked at Sukhi for a while and said, "Let's go there".

While Sukhi was driving, he was very quiet. Priya asked him what was wrong. He replied that there was nothing wrong with him. She asked him again to tell her what had happened. He said he was a little worried now as he felt that that she hadn't come out of the 'Ronny zone' properly. Priya said she needed some more time to come out of that properly as she loved him (Sukhi) more than anyone else.

Sukhi said she could have as much time as she wanted, but, whenever he needed her, she had to come with him. She promised him that she would always stand by him, no matter what was going on around them. Priya then told Sukhi to smile. Sukhi smiled at her and said he could happily die for her. She replied he didn't have to die for her; he had to live with her. Then, she kissed him on the cheek while he was still driving.

When they reached the Indian restaurant, Sukhi opened the car door for Priya and they went inside. They took a corner table for two and sat there. Sukhi pulled out the chair for her, which impressed her a lot. She reminded herself that Ronny had never done this for her; he always taken her for granted. Priya felt very special around Sukhi. The waiter came, they ordered some food. Sukhi asked her if she needed drinks or wine with the starters.

She said she didn't drink wine or alcohol. Sukhi said he didn't drink much too, as he didn't like the taste of alcohol. Priya smiled and said she liked it as she had seen a drunkard at home. While they were waiting for the food to come, Sukhi said he had friends in Sydney and they also wanted to join them but couldn't make it. Priya said she could go over some other time and meet up with his mates.

Then, Priya asked him about his past girlfriends. Sukhi raised his eyebrows and said he had none as he never been in any relationships before, but there were some girls who were his friends but not an affair kind of friends – just casual friends. He said he didn't find a girl yet. Priya raised her eyebrows and said "Yet"

Sukhi said he finally found one – she was sitting next to him. Priya smiled and blushed. Priya said even she hadn't had had any boyfriends; she had been approached by some guys, but nobody was as smart as him. Sukhi said she was making him feel shy, and he started blushing. Priya said she was telling him the truth.

Sukhi asked her to change the topic as he was feeling uncomfortable. Priya smiled and said she wouldn't mind if he praised her. So, Sukhi told her that when he had seen her for the first time, he had fallen for her but she hadn't even noticed him. He had never seen such a beautiful face in his life. Priya said she was flattered and now he could change the topic as she had had enough. He also added that he had been stalking her for so long and thought that she didn't want to be anyone's friend that he was on the edge of giving up. Priya smiled and said everything happened for a reason and this was the best thing that ever happened to her, and she enjoyed being in relationship with him.

While they were talking, the waiter interrupted them and served the food. Sukhi asked her about her hobbies, to which she replied by saying that she had a passion of photography and wanted to buy a new DSLR camera.

Priya then asked Sukhi about his hobbies, to which he replied by saying that he liked to spend time watching movies and travelling and, most importantly, playing video games on play station.

When they finished eating, Sukhi got up and paid for it while Priya waited for him. When they were leaving, Sukhi again opened the door for her and then the car door for her. While they were driving back, Priya said she had had the nicest evening of her life and held Sukhi's hand while he was driving. Sukhi replied that he didn't want her to leave him and kissed her hand. They were both very happy.

Priya said she had always wanted a partner like Sukhi, who was adorable and a gentleman and not like a retard like Ronny. Sukhi said she deserved better than Ronny, so God had sent him (Sukhi) to give her the happiness that she desire. Priya closed her eyes and said she didn't want to wake up now – she wanted to live in her dreams with Sukhi. She was going to plan their future in her dreams.

While Sukhi reached Priya's apartment, Priya fell asleep and Sukhi didn't wake her up as he didn't want to disturb her. He parked his car in the basement of her apartment building. He couldn't stop looking at her. He was enjoying watching her sleep and decided not to wake her up; he would sit there and gaze upon her all night.

After some time, Sukhi also fell asleep. Later, Priya woke up and saw Sukhi sleeping next to her. It was 3 a.m. Now she was looking at Sukhi's face as he was sleeping soundly. It seemed as if she was in her dreams, with him as her husband, and they were enjoying their life without any hassle. She told herself that she didn't want to lose him at any cost and that she would stand by him always.

While she was looking at him, Sukhi opened his eyes slightly and saw that she had woken up and was looking at him. He instantly woke up and asked her why she didn't wake him up when she got up; she said she could ask him the same question. Sukhi smiled and stretched himself and asked her what the time was. She saw her watch and said it was 3:30 a.m. Sukhi said he would go home as he had work in the morning. Priya asked him to stay over since there was no one else at home. She added that Ronny was in Melbourne, and she didn't have any problem if Sukhi could come to her place. Sukhi refused, but Priya insisted that he stay.

They both went to Priya's apartment, and Sukhi went to the bathroom. Priya asked him if he needed anything; Sukhi said a blanket would be fine and he could sleep on the couch. Priya said she wouldn't let him sleep now – they both could stay up all night and talk. Sukhi shouted from the bathroom that he had work in the morning and he had to go to his apartment to change his clothes. Priya chuckled and said she won't let him sleep and laughed. Sukhi then said it was fine, but she had to make him a cup of coffee.

When Sukhi came out of the bathroom, the coffee was ready. He took his cup and sat on the couch while she came on the couch and leaned against him.

Sukhi started to cuddle her and said she was just like a baby. Priya smiled and said she was his baby. They both smiled and Sukhi held her face and kissed her forehead. After that kiss, Priya said the coffee must be really strong and erotic. Sukhi broke into laughter and said yeah might be.

The next morning, Sukhi woke up and saw that they had both slept on Priya's couch. Sukhi didn't wake her up; he went to his own apartment. He was running late for work, so quickly changed and left. Mike was waiting for him outside and asked what took him so long, since he had never come late to work. Sukhi asked him if the boss was there or not. Mike said he hadn't come to work yet; Sukhi breathed a sigh of relief and said he had gotten lucky that day.

They both went inside, and Mike said he hadn't gotten his answer. Sukhi asked him what he wanted to know. Mike again asked where he had been last night as he had gone to Sukhi's apartment but no one had answered the door. Sukhi said he had been with Priya and spent the night at her place. Mike raised his eyebrows; Sukhi nodded and said he had spent a beautiful evening with Priya.

Mike asked if they had decided what to do. Sukhi said that she would talk to her sister about it. If her sister agreed, then they would proceed further. Until she talked to her sister, they had to meet each other on the sly because of Ronny.

Then, Mike went to his cabin and told Courtney to go home. She had been waiting to see Sukhi. Courtney then asked why she had to leave, as she hadn't talked to Sukhi yet. Mike told her that Sukhi was seeing someone else, and that he saw Courtney as a friend and nothing more than that.

Courtney started crying and Mike tried to calm her down. Courtney then asked who the girl was but Mike couldn't tell her as Sukhi had asked him not say anything. Courtney ran outside crying. Mike ran after her, but she told Mike to leave her alone; she wouldn't bother him and Sukhi after that.

Sukhi saw someone running outside in the corridor from his cabin window and then Mike running after that person. When Mike came back, Sukhi was waiting for him outside his cabin. Mike ignored him but Sukhi approached him and asked him who he was running after. Mike didn't say anything and went to his cabin. Sukhi followed him and asked him once again. Mike angrily asked why Sukhi was bothered. Sukhi was shocked and said it was because he was concerned. Mike said it was nothing and asked Sukhi to leave him alone for a bit.

Sukhi said he was not going anywhere until he knew who Mike was running after. Mike raised his voice and said he was running after Courtney; she had gone to his place last night and was worried about Sukhi as he hadn't replied to any of her phone calls or messages for two weeks. Because of that, they had both gone to his apartment the previous night; since he hadn't been home, she had come with Mike to the office this morning to see him.

Sukhi felt very bad and apologised to mike. Mike shouted and said that he had to say sorry to that poor girl who was concerned about him. Sukhi said he would talk to Courtney and tell her that he was not in love with her but they could be friends. Mike gave him an angry look and shouted, "You better talk to her soon…she ran outside crying".

Sukhi felt very bad that Mike was shouting at him. It was not even his fault as he had already mentioned to Courtney that he needed some time to think about their relationship. So, Sukhi asked Mike not to shout at him as it was not his fault. Mike replied that he was not scolding Sukhi – he felt very bad for Courtney as he was the one who had introduced them. Sukhi said that he would talk to her and sort everything out. Mike said he should do it as soon as Sukhi could. He didn't want to see Courtney crying as she was like his sister. Sukhi hugged him and said he would take care of everything and he had nothing to worry about.

Mike said he couldn't understand why Courtney had fallen for Sukhi if he had already mentioned that they could only be friends. Sukhi replied that he too couldn't understand. Then, they both went for lunch.

After Sukhi finished work, he went to McDonalds as usual, and waited at the car park. Priya came after 10 minutes and hugged him and said Ronny was coming tomorrow night. If Sukhi wanted, he could join her for dinner tonight, to which Sukhi smiled and replied that he would be there. He said he had to go to see someone now and he would see her after that. Priya said she would cook the best dinner for him. Sukhi smiled and said he would help her as he knew how to cook.

Sukhi then went to Courtney's place. When Courtney saw Sukhi standing at the door, she started crying and asked why he had come there. Sukhi replied that he was very sorry for past two weeks, but he was there to tell her that they could be friends once again, even though he already knew that Courtney had some feelings for him. Courtney said they couldn't be friends as she wanted to spend her life with him.

Sukhi said he was seeing someone right now and he couldn't promise her that. Courtney started crying again and said if she couldn't have him in her life, nobody else would get him either. Sukhi felt uncomfortable and asked her to stop talking crap.

Courtney shouted, "I will kill that bitch!" Sukhi slapped her and told her to stop saying that as he loved that girl. Courtney started crying bitterly and screamed at him – then, suddenly, she hugged him and said she was not going to leave him until he confessed that too he loved her.

Sukhi tried to push her back but she held him very tightly. Sukhi felt uncomfortable and pushed her back. She fell on the floor and broke down in tears and started crawling on the floor. Sukhi reached to her and tried to comfort her. While he was comforting her, she got up and hugged him tightly and sobbed, "Please don't hate me after this".

Sukhi replied calmly that he was not going to hate her as she was a nice girl. Courtney looked at him with tears in her eyes and asked him to repeat what he said. Sukhi said that she was a nice girl and she could get anyone, but he was in love with Priya so he couldn't be with her. But he would be very happy if she found someone, and they could be friends.

Courtney later calmed down and said it was fine if they could be friends again. Sukhi said he would always be her friend, no matter what had happened between them, and he would be there whenever she needed him. Courtney smiled and said it was good to have him back in her life. Sukhi said that he needed to go to Priya's place and that he would see her later. Courtney asked him that if he could give her a hug before he left. Sukhi smiled and gave her a nice, tight hug and then left.

When Sukhi reached his apartment, he showered and put on a nice shirt and blazer. While he was driving to Priya's house, he stopped at the florist to get her some nice flowers. When he reached at Priya's place, Ronny opened up the door! Sukhi was stunned when he saw Ronny. Ronny asked him who he was looking for. Sukhi couldn't reply at first, and suddenly asked, "Is Courtney home?"

Ronny angrily replied, "You knocked on the wrong door buddy, no Courtney stays here". Sukhi apologised for the inconvenience. Ronny was totally drunk and said

"Piss off man!" Sukhi was offended and said, "Sorry, what did you say?" Ronny turned his face to Sukhi and told him to get the hell out of there before he kicked him out. Sukhi told him to behave himself – if not; he would also knock his head off. Priya was folding her hands from the far end and silently gesturing to him to leave. Sukhi saw that and showed Ronny the middle finger and then left.

Sukhi then went to Mike's place. Mike was surprised to see him and asked about what happened. Sukhi explained everything and said he needed a drink, that's why he had come over. Mike made him a drink and they both went to the balcony. Mike calmed him down and asked him to leave that "prick" out of his (Sukhi) mind as it was not worth it. Sukhi said he felt sorry for Priya. Mike told Sukhi to buy some time to deal with it. As they had to deal with Ronny before going any further with their relationship. Sukhi agreed. Mike told him to stay for dinner.

Sukhi was very quiet during dinner. After dinner, Sukhi was about to go home when he stopped and told Mike about the incident with Courtney. Mike was not impressed with that and said he would talk to her some day. Sukhi thanked him and said he had better go now and have some rest.

Next morning, on his way to work, he stopped at McDonalds. It seemed to have become a habit to stop there every day before and after work. He went inside to talk to Priya about Ronny and ask how he had come back so early from Melbourne, but, unfortunately, Priya wasn't at work as her shift hadn't started yet.

At his workplace, Mike came into Sukhi's cabin and told him that he had talked to Courtney and she was feeling better now. He added that he would like to throw a party at his house for the baby shower – Sukhi was invited and Courtney would also be there. Sukhi said he had to talk to Priya first as he was worried about her. Mike said they could go to McDonalds at lunch, and Sukhi could talk to Priya there.

When they went to McDonalds at lunch time, Priya was at the counter. She had a black spot on her left cheek. Mike gave his order and Sukhi stood next to him. Priya didn't even look at him. Sukhi felt bad and tried to talk to her, but Priya signalled to him that Ronny was sitting there. Sukhi and Mike went to the dine-in area where Ronny was sitting. Sukhi sat at the next table and kept looking at Ronny. Ronny gave him an angry look at which Sukhi showed him the middle finger. Mike broke into laughter and told Sukhi to relax. Sukhi said he was relaxing and Mike had nothing to worry about.

A staff member called out Mike's coupon number for his food. Mike went to collect it and told Priya to keep an eye on them as it looked like they were going to fight here. Priya signalled to Sukhi to stay away from Ronny. Sukhi nodded his head and turned his face to other side. Mike came back and said, "Let's go". While Sukhi was leaving, Priya said she would text him after Ronny left and, then, they could meet.

When Sukhi reached his workplace, he got a text from Priya that Ronny had left. Sukhi replied he couldn't meet now; he would be there after he finished work. Priya replied with a smiley face that she would wait.

Priya was waiting for him at the McDonalds car park. Sukhi hugged Priya and asked what had happened to her. She replied that nothing had happened to her. Sukhi said he could still see the black spot on her left cheek. She replied that she had been beaten up by Ronny after Sukhi had come to her place looking for Courtney, as Ronny thought she had an affair with someone else. Sukhi asked her what she had said about him after that. She replied that she had said that she didn't care. Ronny had thrown a glass he was holding at that time at her, but she had escaped it. He had slapped her several times after that. Sukhi got angry with Ronny, and said he would kill him.

"It seemed to be very hard for him to control his anger."

Priya told him to calm down and said he could come to her place tonight as Ronny was going back to Melbourne. Ronny had come to her workplace to tell her that he was leaving for Melbourne after she finished work, so she could drop him at the airport. Sukhi asked her why Ronny had come back last night. Priya replied that he had some work pending so he had received a call in the morning. Sukhi smiled and said he would bring some medicinal cream to put on her cheek. Priya hugged him and asked him to go as Ronny was coming.

Fate was not on their side – Ronny had seen everything. He called up Priya's brother and told him everything. Priya's brother told him to bring her to India, and do whatever he wanted with Sukhi. Ronny said he would kill him. Priya's brother said he could, and laughed. Ronny hung up the phone and tried to calm down.

After sometime, Ronny went inside the McDonalds and told Priya to come out. Ronny was very angry at her but he couldn't do anything there. When Ronny drove her home, she was surprised as he had told her that he was going to Melbourne. She kept quiet as she assumed that he might have forgotten something at home. When they went to their apartment, Ronny made a big scene and slapped Priya and told her that he had seen everything that had happened between her and Sukhi. He said they were leaving for India the next morning. Priya refused to go with him but Ronny threw a chair at her and slapped her and told her to pack her bags. He went into their bedroom and smashed Priya's phone. He was shouting at Priya while he was looking for his gun, which he had kept in one of the drawers.

Priya was unaware of what Ronny was looking for and she couldn't reply to Sukhi, who was coming to her place that evening. She began crying as she packed her bag. She started praying to God to change Sukhi's mind and stop him from coming to her place. She also that worried that if she went back to India with Ronny, her family would force her to marry Ronny.

Sukhi was unaware of all this and he was getting ready to go to Priya's place in the evening. According to him, Ronny was going to Melbourne and Priya would be at home alone. He was planning to take Priya out to a nice restaurant so that they could enjoy their evening together. After that, they could go to the lake and spend some time there.

While Sukhi was driving to Priya's place, he called Mike and told him that he would be at Priya's place and wouldn't be able to go for the baby shower party. Mike shouted and said he had promised him, so Sukhi apologised and said that Ronny had gone back to Melbourne – that was the only reason Priya had invited him. He added that he might come over with Priya if she didn't mind. Mike agreed and said they had to promise him that they would come to his place, as Keth also wanted to meet Priya. Sukhi replied that he would be there but a little late. Mike said that was fine but he had to make sure that he would come.

Sukhi went to Priya's place and knocked on the door. Nobody opened the door, but when he tried to open it from the outside, the door was not locked and could be opened. He saw that Priya was lying on the floor and Ronny was pointing a gun at him. Sukhi went to Priya and shouted at Ronny, asking what he had done to her. Sukhi turned Priya's face towards him and saw that she was unconscious. He tried to wake her up by calling her name repeatedly and started shouting and screaming for help. Priya slightly opened her eyes and saw Sukhi crying. She wiped his tears and said "Don't cry dear, I am alright". She didn't see that Ronny was holding a gun and that he was drunk.

Ronny then threw a table on Sukhi, and Sukhi fell on the floor. Sukhi got up and pushed him back. Ronny tried to hit Sukhi, but Sukhi went sideways and Ronny slipped and fell on the floor. He was still holding his gun, and, as he pointed it at Sukhi, and unconsciously he pulled the trigger and shot the fire. The bullet stuck Sukhi on the left side of his chest and he fell on top of Ronny.

Ronny flipped Sukhi's body over. Suddenly, Priya opened her eyes and saw Sukhi lying on the floor with blood coming out from his body. He was unconscious and it looked as if he was dead. She ran over reached out to his body and put his head on her lap and started to weep bitterly as she yelled, "Why God? Why did you do this to him? He had done nothing wrong to anybody!" Ronny was drunk and was struggling to walk, but he managed to pull Priya up. He slapped her and asked her to get her bag.

Priya tried to hit him but Ronny was stronger and she couldn't do anything. She tried to shoot herself but the gun was not loaded and she didn't know how to load it. Ronny just laughed cruelly and said the gun was his baby and she didn't need big boy's toys. She cried and hit him, but it was pointless as he was not getting hurt. Ronny got irritated with her behaviour and pointed the gun at her and asked her to get their bags. She asked him to shoot as she didn't want to live any more. He just grabbed their bags and forced Priya to go with him. Priya refused and hugged Sukhi's body, but Ronny forcefully grabbed her and left for the airport.

Sukhi was still breathing but was unable to move. Mike was calling him on his cell phone but Sukhi couldn't pick it up. Mike became anxious and told Keth that he was going to Priya's place to see if everything was fine. Keth asked him why he wanted to go. Mike replied that he had a weird feeling that something was wrong with Sukhi – as he was not picking up his phone and he had never done that before. Keth said she also wanted to go with him but Mike told her to stay at home as his mates would be arriving soon for the baby shower party.

Mike went to Priya's place and knocked on the door. The door opened and he saw Sukhi lying on the floor, covered in blood. Mike touched Sukhi's body and observed that he was still breathing. So he picked him up and went to the hospital. On the way, he called Keth and asked her to come to the hospital. He was crying and sobbing. Keth asked him what had happened, but he couldn't tell her and said that she had to come as soon as possible to the hospital. He would explain everything there.

When they reached the hospital, Mike was crying for help as Sukhi had almost stopped breathing. The hospital staff put Sukhi on a stretcher and took him to the emergency unit. They took him to the operation theatre and team of doctors came to operate on him. Mike was waiting outside, weeping bitterly and praying to God for Sukhi's recovery. He then saw Keth was running in the corridor. Mike waved to her; Keth saw him and ran towards him. Mike then hugged her tightly and started crying again. Keth tried to comfort him and asked him what had happened. Mike sobbingly said that Sukhi had been shot and he was bleeding and unconscious.

After four hours of surgery, the doctor came out from the operation theatre and told Mike to come to his cabin. Mike and Keth followed the doctor to his cabin and sat down. Doctor told him that Sukhi was very lucky that his heart was not hit by the bullet; they had taken the bullet out from his body, but he had lost a lot of blood, and that's why he was still unconscious. They had to keep him in the ICU for the next 24 hours – only after that they could be sure of his condition. In the meantime, if they wanted to meet him, they could only see him through the window.

Mike and Keth stand next to the window and saw Sukhi. They both started sobbing; Mike held Keth's hand and said everything would be alright. Keth wasn't sure if Sukhi would be alright after that. She hugged Mike and said she was bit scared. Mike consoled her and said Sukhi would be alright; he was just sleeping.

After 24 hours, the head doctor went to check Sukhi and told Mike and Keth that Sukhi was out of danger and he would be conscious in a couple of hours. They both breathed a sigh of relief. Keth asked Mike what had happened with Priya. Mike said that when he had gone to her apartment, there was no one there. Mike told Keth to stay at the hospital, so that he could go and check where they had gone. Mike then rushed to Priya's apartment to look for evidence. He saw that all of their belongings were not there, not even their passports. He saw a receipt for booking of air tickets to India, so he assumed that they had gone to India.

On the other hand, Priya and Ronny were on the plane. Priya was weeping and Ronny was drinking. He didn't even bother to console her. Priya was remembering the moments she had spent with Sukhi. They both were thinking that Sukhi was dead. Ronny wanted to get married as soon as they reached home, but Priya was thinking of committing suicide.

When Sukhi got up, he screamed out Priya's name. The doctors tried to calm him down but he kept screaming and shouting Priya's name. Keth was alone there as Mike had gone to find out about Priya. When Sukhi calmed down, the doctors explained that he had been shot. He was seriously injured but Mike had gotten him to the hospital on time and they had saved his life.

Sukhi then asked the doctor how long he had to be in hospital, as he had to find someone and save her. The doctors said it depended on how fast his body recovered. Just then, Mike reached there and saw that Sukhi was conscious. Before entering to the ICU unit, he thanked God for saving Sukhi's life. Sukhi saw Mike standing outside and told the doctors that he wanted to meet Mike.

The doctors came outside and told Mike that Sukhi wanted to see him; they added that Sukhi shouldn't get angry at any cost as his body was still recovering from the blood loss. Mike assured the doctors that he would be careful.

Mike then went inside. Sukhi looked at him and said that he had to go and find Priya. Mike didn't say anything and stood there quietly. After a while, he told Sukhi to take some rest, but Sukhi shouted at him and said he wanted to know about Priya and broke into tears.

Mike then also started crying and said that she had left with Ronny to India – he had gone to her apartment and found the receipt for their air-ticket bookings. Sukhi started weeping and said he also wanted to go India right away. Mike told him to rest and that he would take care of everything. Sukhi then told Mike that he wanted to talk to someone in India and asked for his cell phone.

Mike gave him his phone and Sukhi called his best friend, Mandy, in India. He told Mandy to find Priya for him. Mandy asked Sukhi why he was talking weirdly – Sukhi replied that it was a long story but that he would be in India soon. But before he got there, Mandy had to do something for him. Mandy was surprised and asked him, "What?" Sukhi gave the phone to Mike so that he could explain everything.

Mike took the phone from Sukhi and told Mandy everything that had happened over the past few weeks. Mandy was shocked and asked why he hadn't been informed. Mike told him that Sukhi was supposed to give him a surprise. Mike said that he would send Priya's pictures, and that Mandy had to find her as soon as possible. He also asked him not to tell this to anyone. Mandy asked about Sukhi's family – Mike said he couldn't tell them as well. Mike then hung up the phone and sent Mandy a picture of Priya.

After two weeks, Mandy called Sukhi and told him that he had found Priya – she was fine, but she thought Sukhi was dead. Sukhi told Mandy not to tell Priya that he was alive. He would be in India by next week, and then they would go and save her from Ronny. Mandy agreed and said he would keep an eye on Priya to make sure she was safe until Sukhi got there.

Mike told Sukhi that he also wanted to go with him to India. Sukhi refused, saying he didn't want him to get into any trouble as in India anything can happen to him (Sukhi) and he didn't want to involve Mike in his fight. Mike begged him, saying he couldn't let Sukhi go alone.

Sukhi told him that Keth was pregnant and she needed him there with her. Mike started crying and said he wanted to be with him so that Sukhi could be safe. Sukhi finally agreed and told him to book the tickets as soon as possible. Mike then told him that he had already booked the tickets while he was still recovering.

The day before their departure, Sukhi was discharged from the hospital. Sukhi got home and started to pack his bags when he got a call from Mandy saying that Priya had tried to run away from her house. Her family had caught her and now she couldn't get out of the house. Sukhi got shocked and asked why she had tried to run away – without her help, they couldn't do anything. Mandy told him that she didn't know that Sukhi was still alive, and added that he knew her best friend now and they could get help from her to get in touch with Priya.

Sukhi appreciated Mandy's help and told him his flight details and asked someone to clean his family house there. Mandy said he would be there to pick him up, and that he would send someone to clean his house.

Sukhi then called up his parents and told them everything. His father was very upset as he hadn't told them about this situation, and wanted to go to India to help him out but Sukhi refused saying it was his fight and he had to do it alone. If everything went well, he would be home with Priya. His father said he wouldn't tell his mother anything but Sukhi had to keep him updated.

Sukhi packed his bag and stayed over at Mike's place. Keth also wanted to go with them but she couldn't travel as she was pregnant. Keth was upset when they were both leaving, and she told them to come back a winner. Sukhi hugged her and thanked her for the support as that really mattered to him – they were his family in Australia. Mike said that they too considered Sukhi as family and would do anything for him. That's why he wanted to go with him to India to save Priya – he considered it his duty and right to protect his family and he would continue to do that.

After that, they enjoyed their dinner and went for sleep. Sukhi got up at midnight and cried for help to God, and asked for the courage to stand up for his love. He knew it wouldn't be easy to fight against a society that believes in caste and religion. In India, marrying outside one's caste is against society and God's will. But Sukhi was all set to stand against those odds for his love.

Before leaving for the airport, Sukhi hugged Keth and went down very quickly as he wanted Mike to spend some time with Keth, as he had never left her alone before.

While driving to airport, Sukhi was very quiet as he was thinking of all the memories he had in Australia. If everything went well in India, he would shift to America with Priya and wouldn't return to Australia. Meanwhile, Mike was thinking of getting a bigger house so that they could all live together as a family.

At the airport, Sukhi stood in the line; Mike weighed the baggage and then joined Sukhi in the queue. They got their boarding passes and left for their gate from where they were to board the aircraft.

On the plane, Sukhi ordered some juice while Mike was more interested in the alcohol. But Sukhi refused him to drink as they had to make some plans, and he had to be strong as it would be very hot in India. Mike replied that he would be happy when Priya could be with them. Sukhi then smiled and agreed to have one drink, Mike. Mike smiled and said "Cheers!"

While they were on the plane, Sukhi fell asleep and dreamt that Priya was running towards him. All around Priya were some buildings; the buildings were on fire and she was in the middle of the road. Sukhi was lying on the ground in a pool of blood. They were all alone. Sukhi cried in his sleep and Mike got worried. He woke Sukhi up and consoled him.

Mike asked him what had happened, to which Sukhi replied that he had had the worst nightmare of his life. Mike chuckled and said he thought Sukhi had gone mad after getting shot. They both then laughed and Sukhi went back to sleep.

They reached New Delhi airport at around 8p.m. When they came out, Sukhi saw Mandy waiting for them. Sukhi hugged Mandy and said it was good to see him. Mandy shook hands with Mike and said, "Welcome to India".

Mike smiled and hugged him and said it was good to meet him. Mandy looked weirdly at him and said he didn't expect him to be so friendly after that phone call. Mike said he hadn't seen him properly yet. Sukhi looked at him and Mike zipped up his lips. Mandy then took them to the car park.

On the way home, Mike and Sukhi said they were hungry. Mandy told them to wait – once they hit the highway, they could stop at the one of the dhabas (Indian name for pit-stop restaurants on the Highway).

Mandy stopped outside a dhaba and ordered some food for all of them. He asked Sukhi how he was feeling. Sukhi replied sadly that he would be better when Priya was safe and secure. Mandy said that Priya was not allowed to come out of her house, and that they would have to sneak in. Sukhi said it was not a good idea – if they got caught, everything would be ruined. Mike said they had to beat Ronny up for what he had done to Sukhi, and they had to do it without Sukhi being seen – if not, it would mean more trouble to Priya.

Sukhi agreed and said that they had to teach Ronny a lesson. Mandy asked how they were going to do it. Sukhi told Mandy that Ronny was an arrogant person – if they could irritate him somehow, he would try to fight back. At that time, they had to beat him up. Mandy said he could ask his friends to do that.

Mike said he won't be doing this with Mandy – if Ronny saw his face he might get an idea that why he got beaten up. Mandy agreed. They finished their food and hit the road once again.

They reached Sukhi's house early in the morning. They were all tired. Sukhi told Mandy to stay over and get some rest as he was driving all the way through. Mandy agreed and they all went to sleep. Before going to bed, they had a couple of drinks and they all raised a toast for Sukhi and Priya.

Sukhi woke up in the afternoon, but Mike and Mandy were still sleeping. Sukhi woke them up and said he was ready, and they had only half-an-hour to get ready. Mandy asked where they were going. Sukhi said he wanted to see Priya, so they were going to her town to meet her best friend. Mandy gave him the best friend's contact number and said that, while they were getting ready, he could call her. Mandy had already told her about the two of them.

Sukhi called Priya's friend, Shilpa. When she picked up her phone, Sukhi told her he had arrived in India and he would like to see her that evening. Shilpa said that she would try to ask Priya's parents if they could allow Priya to go outside for a little while. Sukhi said it would be much appreciated if she could do that as he was dying to see Priya, but he asked Shilpa not to tell her that he was alive – he wanted to give Priya a surprise. Shilpa added that Priya had told her over the phone that she had fallen in love with a guy in Australia, and she (Shilpa) was helping them just because she wanted Priya to be happy.

Sukhi replied that he appreciated her help and that he would be there soon, and would give her a call once he got there. Sukhi hung up the phone and saw that Mandy was not ready yet. He yelled out at him and told him to be quick. Mandy said it was Mike's fault as he took too long to use the washroom. When he saw Mike's face, he started laughing as Mike had almost fainted when he pointed at him. Sukhi told him to hurry up as they were getting late.

After lunch, they hit the road. After an hour's drive, they reached Priya's town and Sukhi called Shilpa to let her know that he was there. Shilpa was excited as she was sitting next to Priya in her house. She asked Priya to go out with her, but Priya refused as she was very sad. Shilpa insisted and said that if she went out with her, she would feel better. Priya said her brother wouldn't allow that. Shilpa said she would ask her brother.

Shilpa went to Priya's brother, who was sitting in the study room, and told him that Priya was feeling very low and asked if she could take Priya to the park to cheer her up. It would be beneficial for them if she could come out of that grief easily. She promised to bring her back safely. Her brother agreed that and said it would be much better if Shilpa could convince her to marry Ronny. Shilpa went back to Priya's room and told her to get ready as they were going to the park. While Priya was in the bathroom, she saw that Ronny had heard everything, so she texted Sukhi that Ronny might be there to keep an eye on Priya as he had heard them talking about going to the park. Sukhi then changed the plan – she had to come to the restaurant with Priya. Mandy and his friends would take care of Ronny at the park.

Sukhi told Mandy that Ronny had heard their plan and he would follow them to the park. From the park, they would run to the restaurant where Mandy and his friends would take care of Ronny. Mandy got out the car in anger and said he would take care of everything. Sukhi added that Ronny would come to them to argue and they just had to gather some crowd so that Priya and Shilpa could flee from there. Mandy agreed and left.

When Shilpa and Priya reached the park, Mandy saw them and texted Shilpa to sit on a bench. Shilpa did so, and they sat on a bench in the middle of the park. Ronny and his mate were roaming at the back of the park to keep an eye on them. When Ronny was alone for a moment, Mandy went and bumped into him on purpose. Ronny saw him doing it on purpose and shouted abuses at him. Mandy got angry and they exchanged some swear words but Ronny didn't get into a fight as he had to keep an eye on Priya and Shilpa. Mandy observed that and then he purposely slapped Ronny, and Mandy and his mates surrounded Ronny.

Ronny tried to flee but Mandy and his friends beat him up badly. A crowd gathered there and tried to stop them from fighting but it was too late. Ronny and his friends were sent to hospital as they were brutally beaten up by Mandy and his friends.

On the other hand, Shilpa and Priya left the park and went to the restaurant where Sukhi and Mike were waiting for them. Priya was still unaware about Sukhi could be there. When Priya saw Sukhi sitting there, she couldn't believe that he was alive! She assumed that she was imagining him, but when Shilpa went to meet Sukhi and shook hands with him, she knew that Sukhi was alive and she hugged him tightly. She wept bitterly and kept saying that she loved him and that she was sorry for everything that happened in Australia. Sukhi told her to stop crying as he was going to take her to be with him forever.

Priya then looked up at him and asked him sobbingly what he would do. Sukhi smiled and said he would make everything perfect for them and they would live happily ever after. Priya said she would never leave him alone now, and that she would stand by his side always. Sukhi smiled and hugged her again. When they were about to settle down, Mandy entered the restaurant and shouted that he had taken care of Ronny. Priya and Shilpa looked at him strangely and asked him what he had done with Ronny. Mandy shook his head and said that he and his friends had taken care of him, such that Ronny wouldn't be able to walk properly for about two or three months. So, there would be no wedding pressure on Priya. Priya and Shilpa jumped with joy and hugged each other.

Mandy then asked Sukhi about his plans. Sukhi said he had to talk to Priya's brother and convince him about their marriage. Priya shouted and said this was very bad idea as her brother would never approve of their relationship. Sukhi held her hand and said he had to talk to her brother as he was the only one who had influence over her family, and her brother would decide whom Priya had to marry. Priya was worried at first, but agreed later.

Sukhi said they had to find someone who would help them approach her brother and who could fix a meeting between them. Shilpa said that she knew someone who could help them. She knew a guy called Vicky, who used to work for Monty, Priya's Brother. Vicky used to work in a computer centre that was owned by Monty. Sukhi said he could consider Vicky only if he would actually help them. Shilpa said that she and Vicky was a couple, and he would definitely help them. Sukhi agreed and said he wanted to meet him as soon as possible.

Shilpa then called Vicky and asked him to come to the restaurant. While they were waiting for Vicky, Priya got a text message from Monty saying that Ronny was in the hospital and the wedding would be postponed for about a month, but the exact date depended on when Ronny would be discharged from the hospital. Priya and Shilpa jumped with joy.

When Vicky arrived at the restaurant, Shilpa introduced him to everyone and said that she needed a favour from him. Vicky smiled at her and said he could do anything for her. Shilpa blushed and Sukhi interrupted them and said "Hey love birds, please concentrate!" Everyone laughed at that. Shilpa explained everything to Vicky and convinced him to help them.

Sukhi then made a plan with Vicky and said they would meet Monty the next day in the evening at the same place. Vicky had to convince Monty to come there without any of his mates. Later, Vicky would go to the toilet and, at that point of time, Sukhi would come and sit next to Monty and talk to him. Vicky liked the idea. Sukhi added that after his meeting with Monty, Priya could have a hard time with him at home and she had to maintain her stand in front of everybody now. After that, everyone decided to leave. Sukhi and Priya again hugged each other and everyone else turned their backs so that they could share a private moment.

Later, when they were going back to their homes, Sukhi got a text message from Shilpa – she wrote that Vicky had spoken to Monty to meet up at the restaurant; Monty agreed and said he would be there. Sukhi was delighted and thanked her for all her efforts. Shilpa replied with a smiley face that she would do anything for Priya.

Mike and Mandy had been to a liquor store. When they came back, Sukhi showed them the text message that he got from Shilpa. Mike and Mandy shouted with joy.

Mandy said the celebration would be more delightful now, and that they would enjoy it near a pond in his town, where Mandy and Sukhi had some sweet memories. Mandy then tried to scare Mike by saying that he had to be cautious as there would be wild animals near that pond. Mike got scared but Sukhi told him not to worry as Mandy was just joking, and there would be no one except them.

Mandy then said they would take some food and light a fire and enjoy to the fullest. Mandy stopped at the dhaba again and ordered some food to carry at the pond. While Mandy was ordering the food, Sukhi got a message from Shilpa. It was a snap of all of them when they were waiting at the restaurant for Vicky. Sukhi showed it to Mike and Mandy and emotionally hugged both of them and thanked them for what they were doing for him. Mandy said Sukhi didn't have to mention it as he was like a brother to him and he would do anything for him. Mike agreed with Mandy.

They took their food, grabbed some firewood and went to the pond. Sukhi lit the fire and Mandy put out the drinks. They talked about childhood memories and laughed and had a nice time. The next morning, Sukhi woke up and saw that Mike and Mandy were still sleeping. He didn't bother to wake them up, as he wanted to go to the temple and pray for energy and strength to face Priya's family and a society that is against inter-caste marriage. He went to temple and prayed, and spent some time there.

While he was there, Sukhi saw a beggar standing outside. He was very skinny. Sukhi asked him why he was standing outside – why not go inside to have some food and shelter? The beggar told Sukhi that he was not allowed to go inside the temple as he was from a lower caste. Sukhi took his hand and took him inside the temple. While doing this, another man told Sukhi not to take the beggar inside as it was against society's rules and, moreover, he was not from a general caste as well. Sukhi ignored him and made the beggar stand in the line where food was being served and stood next to him.

Some others yelled at Sukhi for making a beggar stand next to them. Sukhi replied he was a friend of his, and he was not a beggar. Sukhi said he and the beggar were from the same caste. Another man yelled at him and asked him his caste. Sukhi smiled and said, "Humanity". The men shouted abuses at Sukhi and warned him to take the beggar away from that temple, if he didn't do that then it would be bad for him also but Sukhi ignored them and stood there quietly.

The crowd gathered there and everyone was against Sukhi but Sukhi didn't care and then the beggar started to walk away and went outside. He politely said that he didn't want him (Sukhi) to get into any trouble so he was going to stand outside the temple.

Sukhi went to the crowd and asked one guy which caste he belonged to. He replied haughtily that he belonged to a general caste. Sukhi then asked him if he had asked God that he wanted to born in that general caste specifically. The guy was embarrassed and put his head down. Sukhi then asked another guy from the crowd the same question. Everyone put their heads down in shame. Sukhi scolded them, saying that God had created humanity; it was humans who created castes. If they were stopping someone from going to a temple to pray, God would not listen to their prayers as well. The beggar praised Sukhi for his help and he was served food and given shelter there.

When Sukhi came back from the temple, Mike was up but Mandy was still sleeping. Sukhi woke Mandy up and showed him the time – it was almost afternoon. Mandy got up and went to the bathroom to get ready, and Sukhi went to the kitchen where Mike was preparing coffee. Mike was busy preparing coffee and Sukhi was busy preparing himself to face Priya's brother. Mike saw that Sukhi was looking worried. Mike asked Sukhi not to worry about anything. Sukhi said he was worrying about Priya as he didn't want her to get into any kind of trouble. Mike asked him what kind of trouble he was expecting which could happen to Priya. Sukhi replied that she might get beaten up by her elder brother or family. Mike was shocked to hear that and said this was not humane as, in India; women were given the name 'pride of the nation'. How could they do that to her then? Sukhi nodded and said some Indians were not protecting their culture, instead they spoilt it.

Mike also became worried for Priya, and he really wanted to help her out. Sukhi said he couldn't live without her, and now they had to be more careful as it was a delicate situation.

When Mandy was ready, they left for Priya's town. On the way, Mandy asked Sukhi if he could stop for a moment as he was hungry. Mike also said he needed to use the toilet. Sukhi told them to stop at one of the dhabas, but they had to be very quick. Sukhi sat in the car as he was on the phone with Vicky, discussing their plans.

When they reached their destination, Mandy stopped at one of the biggest restaurants in town as there would be a big crowd there, and Monty wouldn't be able to do anything silly. So they sat on the bench opposite the restaurant and waited for Monty and Vicky.

While they were waiting, Sukhi got a call from Vicky. He told Sukhi that Monty was upset about what had happened to Ronny the previous day. Sukhi replied and said he was not scared of him but he was worried if Priya would be in trouble if anything happened between Sukhi and Monty. Vicky said Shilpa would take care of Priya and Sukhi had nothing to worry about; he had to stay calm while he talked to Monty. Sukhi replied that he would be calm, and hung up the call.

Vicky arrived but Monty was not there with him. When Sukhi asked him, he said Monty was on the way. Sukhi told him to go inside and book a table for two and wait for Monty. Sukhi then went back to the same bench where he was sitting before Vicky got there.

Monty came in his car, parked in front of the restaurant and went inside. While he was going in, he saw Sukhi and his friends sitting outside. Monty gave them an angry look and Sukhi responded with the same. They were staring each other like they would get into a fight, but Mike came in between and stood in front of Sukhi and told him not to respond that way as it would be bad for their conversation. Sukhi listened to Mike and put his head down.

Monty went inside, and went towards Vicky. Vicky got up and shook hands with him, and Monty asked him why he had called him there; Vicky could have come home to talk to him. Vicky said he wanted to ask him something about his job. While Vicky tried to get Monty involved in the conversation, he got a text message from Sukhi saying that he was coming inside. Vicky texted him back and asked him to stay outside for a while; he needed more time to assure Monty that he (Vicky) had called him (Monty) for a specific job purpose.

After half-an-hour, Sukhi got a message from Vicky that he would soon go to the toilet and Sukhi could come inside. Sukhi confidently entered the restaurant and saw that Vicky was sitting there. Sukhi and his friends then sat at a table facing Monty's back. From there they could also listen to their conversation. After a little while, Vicky asked Monty to order some food and said that he was going to the toilet. When Vicky left, Sukhi got up and sat next to Monty.

Monty gave him a strange look and asked who was he and why he was sitting at a table that was already occupied by his friend. Sukhi extended his hand for a handshake and said that his name was Sukhi and he had come from Australia. Monty raised his eyebrows and shook hands with him, but said he was expecting someone else. Sukhi said he wouldn't take much of his time – he just wanted to ask him something.

Monty surprisingly asked him what he wanted to ask him. Sukhi said it was something very important. Monty again raised his eyebrows and told him to ask. Sukhi then said that Priya and he had fallen in love with each other. He wanted to ask Monty's permission to marry Priya, instead of her getting married with Ronny.

Monty shook his head angrily and said it was not possible, and Sukhi should leave there before he lost his temper. Sukhi sat quietly for a bit. Then, Monty asked if it was him that Ronny had shot in Australia. Sukhi nodded and said that Ronny had tried to kill him but Priya's love had kept him alive. Monty chuckled and asked him about his caste. Sukhi replied that he belonged to the Brahmin caste. Monty then raised his voice and said how the hell he had asked for Priya's hand when he knew that he was not from their caste. Sukhi calmly replied that he was also a Hindu – the religion Monty and his family belonged to.

Monty shouted that he was a Rajput, and he was proud of it – the person who would marry Priya should be from the same caste. Sukhi then politely asked him if that was the case even if that Rajput boy would be useless for his sister. Monty said Sukhi didn't have to worry about his family as Monty was capable of taking care of them. Sukhi raised his voice and said that he loved her and he would do anything to get her. Monty got up and slapped Sukhi hard. Sukhi was insulted and he angrily grabbed Monty by the collar, but then he (Sukhi) realised that Monty could hurt Priya very badly if he did something to Monty. So he left Monty alone. Mike and Mandy wanted to come in between them but Sukhi refused with his gesture.

Sukhi again asked Monty that he had to think once again about Priya's happiness as she also loved him. Monty looked him in the eye and told him to leave; otherwise he wouldn't be able to walk on his feet. Sukhi stood there for a bit and then walked past him, but, while going outside, Sukhi turned back and held Monty by his neck and said that if he did something to Priya, it would be bad for him – even worse than Ronny, as they were the one who had beaten up Ronny. Monty was shocked as he didn't know that they were those guys who had beaten Ronny up.

Mandy came in between them and pulled Sukhi away; Mandy got worried that Sukhi was about to get involved in a fight with Monty. They all left the place.

Sukhi was very angry and couldn't calm himself down. Mandy called up Shilpa and told her everything, and specially mentioned that Priya should be more cautious. He asked her to look after Priya. Mike took the wheel and drove them to the river.

When they were at the river, Mandy said he was not happy with what happened at the restaurant as he thought that they should have retaliated for Monty's behaviour. Mike interrupted Mandy and said what Sukhi had done was enough for Monty, especially Sukhi had mentioned about Ronny and, now, Monty knew it could happen to him as well.

On the other hand, Monty was angry at Vicky as he thought that there was some connection between Vicky and Sukhi. But Vicky was more cautious and asked Monty about who that guy (Sukhi) in the restaurant was. Monty told him that his name was Sukhi and that he and Priya loved each other. He added that Sukhi had pleaded with him to call off Ronny's and Priya's wedding.

Surprised, Vicky asked him what he thought about that. Monty replied it was not possible as Sukhi was from a different caste. If they were married, society would ignore them and their family would have to leave that town. Vicky said that he had nothing to do with Monty's family matters, but if Priya loved Sukhi then there was a good chance that he would be perfect for her. Monty refused and said he would never allow inter-caste marriages – Priya had to marry Ronny.

Vicky tried his level best, but he couldn't do much about it as he was also an outsider. They had to think of someone else who could convince his family. Monty dropped Vicky at the bus station and went home. While Vicky was waiting for his bus to arrive, he called Shilpa and told her to go to Priya's house as soon as possible. After that he called up Sukhi and told him that he needed to see him immediately.

Sukhi told Mandy to pick Vicky up and grabbed something to drink and eat, as he needed some drinks to calm himself down. Mike said he also needed a drink and went with Mandy. Sukhi was at the riverside, all alone, thinking of something else to get his love back in his life.

On the other hand, when Monty went home, he rushed to Priya's room and saw that she was reading *Love Story* by Erich Segal. Monty threw the book out of the window and told her not to read those silly love stories. Priya felt very bad and asked him what was wrong. Monty asked her about Sukhi. Priya courageously told him that Sukhi was the guy whom she loved and wanted to spend her whole life with. Monty slapped her hard, and the echo of that slap spread through the whole house. He shouted at her and said she had to marry within her caste, and that she had no other option. But Priya didn't lose her confidence and said Sukhi was better than Ronny and she would die rather than marry Ronny.

Just then, her mother interfered and asked them what had happened and why he was beating Priya. Monty told her everything and said she wanted to marry some guy who was not from their caste. He added that she didn't want to marry Ronny. Her mother kept quiet for a while and then sat next to Priya and asked her why she didn't want to marry Ronny. Priya then told her everything about Ronny's nature and how he had behaved with her in Australia, and said she would rather die than marry Ronny. Her mother told Monty to go out as she needed time alone with Priya. Monty shouted that Priya better be ready to marry Ronny, otherwise he would kill everyone and hang himself to death.

Priya and her mother were scared by Monty's threat. Priya cried and said she wanted to marry Sukhi as she couldn't live without him. Her mother opened one of the drawers and took out a bottle of rat poison and gave it to her. Priya asked what she had to do with the poison. Her mother replied that she could marry Sukhi on only one condition: She could either drink this poison or give it to them and then get married to Sukhi.

At that moment, Priya was thinking about Sukhi and all the happy moments she spent with him. At that moment, Priya wanted to die but she wanted to die in Sukhi's arms but her family didn't give her enough time. At that moment, she had to choose between death and Sukhi.

Priya held the bottle in her hand for a while, then screamed Sukhi's name and opened the bottle and drank the liquid. But she didn't die because it was not poison but water in that bottle. Her mother wanted to see who Priya would choose – Sukhi or her family. Priya's mother started crying because she chose Sukhi. Then, her mother hugged her and started trying another tactic – emotional blackmail. She folded her hands in front of Priya and asked her to help them out as they had to live with Monty. If she refused Ronny, then Monty would throw them out of the house. Her mother added that Priya could live with Sukhi after that, but where would they go if Monty threw them out? So they had no option – and that's why she was begging her.

While her mother was trying to convince Priya, Shilpa entered the room and saw her mother pleading with her to accept Ronny. When her mother saw Shilpa, she went to her and pleaded with her to convince Priya to marry Ronny.

Shilpa went to Priya and hugged her very tight and said she needed to stop crying. Priya couldn't stop crying. She was murmuring that she had once lost Sukhi in her life and she didn't want to lose him again. She couldn't live without him. Shilpa then told her that Monty had refused to accept Sukhi because of he was from a different caste. Priya begged Shilpa to help her meet Sukhi right away. Shilpa refused and said she couldn't do that for her, as Monty had doubts that Vicky had a connection with Sukhi. Moreover, he knew that Shilpa and Vicky was a couple.

Priya said she wanted to meet Sukhi – if not, she would kill herself. Shilpa consoled her and said she had to think of Sukhi before doing anything silly like that. Sukhi came a long way just to take her with him and Sukhi also loved her. Priya sobbed and said that she didn't want to marry Ronny. Shilpa said she was also helpless. Then she stood up and told her that she was leaving to meet Sukhi as she was also worried for him. Shilpa added that she would let Priya know about Sukhi. Priya asked her to call when she met Sukhi, as she wanted to hear his voice. Shilpa nodded and left.

When Shilpa went outside, she couldn't stop crying. Shilpa called Sukhi and told him that she wanted to meet him; Sukhi had to come to the riverside as she was heading that way. Sukhi told her that he was already at the riverside, and he would see her soon. When Shilpa reached, Sukhi ran to her and asked if Priya was alright. Shilpa broke into tears and hugged him and said Priya was in trouble. She told him about what had happened – she added that she had tried to calm Priya down, but she was out of control and needed his support.

Sukhi replied intensely and said he was always with her, and he would never leave her in any situation. He shed some tears and turned his face away to hide his tears from Shilpa. Shilpa saw that and said that Priya was very lucky to have him in her life. Sukhi refused and said that Priya was not lucky to have him in her life, as she didn't deserve to be in a situation where she had to choose between him and her family. Sukhi added that fate was not on his side, but he would fight against all odds to get Priya in his life. Shilpa said that she had to leave – if someone saw her there, it could mean trouble for Priya and herself.

Sukhi waited for Mike and Mandy to come. When they arrived, Mandy saw that Shilpa was rushing to her car. They asked Sukhi what had happened. Sukhi told them that the situation was out of control, and they had to do something before Monty and his family did something silly to Priya.

Mike asked him that what they could do to Priya – surely they couldn't kill her. Vicky replied that they could do anything to protect their image in society; if they needed to kill her, they would do it without any hesitation. Moreover, they would be regarded as being 'civilised' if they did something like that to protect their religion and caste values. Mike was shocked on hearing that and asked Sukhi what he wanted to do next.

Sukhi said that he would have to talk to her parents as they were the only ones left to talk to. Mandy said this had to done by some elders; as Sukhi's parents were not there, he would ask his dad to call her father. They could only hope that would help. Sukhi said this was a good idea, but this would be their last chance. If they didn't agree after that, they would have to make some harsh decisions.

Vicky then asked him that what he wanted to do if they still didn't agree. Sukhi shook his head and said he didn't know yet, but he definitely wouldn't agree on running away like a coward. Vicky nodded and said it wouldn't be nice for the families either. They left from the place and dropped Vicky at his place on the way.

While they reached their hometown, Sukhi told Mandy to talk to his father and come back to his place. Mandy said he was bit scared but he would talk to his father at any cost. Sukhi and Mike dropped him at his house and went to their place. Mandy entered the house and saw that his father was sitting on the couch and watching news, so he went to the kitchen and asked his mother about his father's mood. His mother told him that his father's mood was fine but he had some important meeting the next day, so he didn't want anyone to disturb him.

Mandy then slowly went to his father and touched his feet and said he wanted to talk to him about something. His father took a long breath and asked him what had happened. Mandy said nothing had happened to him but he wanted to ask him about his friend, Sukhi. His father looked at him and told him to speak. Mandy said Sukhi was in love with someone. His father looked at him angrily and turned off the TV. Mandy got scared and muttered that he needed his father's help. His father asked him how he could help Sukhi. Mandy told his father everything, and his father replied that he would help him. Mandy jumped with joy and kissed his father's cheek and ran outside.

When Mandy reached Sukhi's house, he shouted to them that his father had agreed to help them out. Sukhi was overwhelmed by his friends' efforts and broke into tears. Mandy hugged him and said that, now, everything depended on Priya's family and how they would respond to his father's call. Sukhi said they would hope for the best – otherwise, he was left with only one option, and that option was against his principles.

The next morning, Sukhi called Shilpa to ask for Priya's father's phone number. She said she didn't have it but she knew the home landline number. Sukhi replied that the landline was not a secure option as Monty could also pick up the call and he could even refuse to talk to Mandy's father also. She said that she would ask Priya and then after she would let him know. After an hour, Shilpa called and gave Sukhi the phone number. She added that Priya was felling a bit better since last night and she could also hope for the best. Sukhi then give the number to Mandy, who passed it on to his father.

Mandy's father called the number and Priya's mother picked up the phone. Mandy's father told her his name and said he wanted to talk to Priya's father. Her mother replied that he was in the washroom and he could call later. Mandy's father felt bad as she was bit rude while talking to him.

After an hour, Mandy's father again called the number and, again, her mother picked up the phone. His father told her that he wanted to talk to her husband, but Priya's mother asked what he wanted to talk to him. Mandy's father then said that he was Sukhi's father, and he wanted to talk to him about Priya's and Sukhi's relationship. Priya's mother angrily replied that it would never happen. Mandy's father asked her why she was saying this without her husband's consent. She rudely replied that they were not from their caste, and they wouldn't agree to an inter-caste marriage. Mandy's father then told her that the kids were in love and they would be happy together – moreover they didn't know any caste and religion. She said that she didn't believe in love, and she wouldn't agree as her son wouldn't agree to it either. He would kill Sukhi and Priya. Priya's mother angrily put the phone down. Mandy's father was furious. He called her once again but she didn't pick up the phone. Mandy's father felt insulted, and he called Mandy and told him what had happened.

Mandy conveyed it to Sukhi. Sukhi was disappointed and wanted to be alone. Sukhi went to the pond and wanted to stay there for a while. On the other side, Priya's family was giving her a hard time. Her mother was emotionally trying to change her mind, and her brother was threatening her with harsh words. Her mother said that Ronny was also a nice guy from a good background. Also, he was Monty's wife's brother, and, if she refused to marry him, it would affect his brother's marriage as well.

Priya responded that Ronny was not a nice guy, and he only wanted a citizenship in Australia – that's why they were forcing her to marry him. Monty got angry. He picked up her laptop and threw on the floor, and said that if she wanted to marry Sukhi he would kill them both. He would forget that she was his sister.

Monty added that he would do anything to protect his and his family's image in society. Priya pleaded and asked why they didn't understand that she wouldn't be happy with Ronny and that she would die at once rather than marry Ronny. Her mother said she would forget about Sukhi once she married Ronny, and that they would have a better future.

Priya wept bitterly and pleaded for mercy, and said she would die if she didn't marry Sukhi. Her mother and brother locked her up in the room and went outside. Shilpa came to their house and asked about Priya. Her mother pleaded with Shilpa to help them, as she was the only person they could trust now. Shilpa refused and said she also thought Sukhi was a nice guy, and they would have to understand that Priya would be happy only with Sukhi.

Monty slapped Shilpa and told her to leave their house immediately. Shilpa slapped Monty back and said he was a coward who was trying to be a nice guy in society, but he was a puppet in his wife's hands inside his house – If he had guts, he would face Sukhi by himself.

Monty went inside his room and picked up his gun and left the house angrily. Shilpa ran outside and called Sukhi and told him to be cautious as Monty was looking for him, and he had just left his house with a gun. Sukhi was at the pond, and told Shilpa to tell Monty to come there. Shilpa told Sukhi to leave immediately as he was in danger. Sukhi smiled and said he was not a coward, and he would wait there for Monty and talk to him. Shilpa pleaded and said he had to think about Priya. Sukhi replied that he was thinking of Priya and he would talk to Monty on his own now. Sukhi also added that Monty was only coming to him because he couldn't control Priya and now he wanted to throw him out of his family's way completely.

Shilpa understood that she couldn't convince Sukhi and did what Sukhi told her to do. She called Monty and told him where to go. She then started praying for everything to be alright, and then called Mandy also who was at Sukhi's home with Mike. She told him that Sukhi might be in danger. Mandy replied that if Monty did anything to Sukhi then he wouldn't be alive. They had had enough of his society and caste system crap.

Monty reached the pond and saw Sukhi sitting under a tree. Sukhi was all alone, while Monty was with a gang of friends. Sukhi saw Monty and stood up. Monty shouted at Sukhi and said he was there to give him option – if he left the country, he would spare him; if he didn't; he would kill him right away. Sukhi said he was not scared of death and, if he had to leave the country, it would be with Priya.

Monty raised his voice and told Sukhi to shut up and he said he didn't want to kill him but he had no option left. Monty's friend came in between and started beating Sukhi. Sukhi struggled at first but later he was on his knees and Monty's friends were holding him tightly. Monty pulled out his gun and pointed it at Sukhi's head. Sukhi's face was covered with blood as Monty's friend had beaten him up very badly. Sukhi held his gun and told Monty to shoot him on the chest where his heart was. If he shot him on his head, he wouldn't get his sister back as Priya lived in his heart and he had to shoot him there. Monty realised that their love for each other were stronger than his strength, but he had no option left as he couldn't kill his sister. If he killed Sukhi, he had a chance of convincing his sister to marry Ronny as Sukhi was no longer in her life. Monty then pleaded with him to go away; he didn't want to kill him, but he would do it to save his family's image in front of society.

Sukhi told him to shoot him before anyone got there, as he didn't want anyone else to see him dying. If not, society would consider Monty as a bad man and Sukhi didn't want that – whatever Monty was doing, he was doing it for his family and society. Then Sukhi yelled at him to shoot– he didn't want to be part of a society where there was no place for love and humanity.

Monty then shot Sukhi in his heart and there were tears in his eyes while shooting him to death. Sukhi smiled at him and touched his heart. Blood was coming out from his chest. He softly murmured, "There you go Monty, now you can have your sister," and fell down on the ground. Monty wept bitterly and kneeled down next to Sukhi's body. His friends picked him up and took him to the car and rushed back to their town.

On the other side, after Shilpa called Mandy, she ran to Priya's room. It was locked from inside. Shilpa knocked on the door but there was no response. When she forced open the door, she couldn't believe her eyes – Priya had hanged herself from the roof and she was dead. Shilpa shouted for help. Priya's mother ran towards her and saw Priya's dead body hanging from the roof. There was a suicide note on the table, which read:

"I respect all religions and caste systems, but I loved Sukhi even more. If Sukhi can't be my husband, then I choose not to live. To hell with this society and caste system that ruined my happiness. Ronny could be a nice person according to you but I had enough of him, and death was an easy choice for me rather than living with Ronny. Society should only be a part of our life not the ruler of our lives. Since childhood, I was listening to the statement that 'God is One' but I had never seen it to be true in my whole life. If there was only one God, how could Sukhi be from outer caste? If religions were there for our benefit, how could they separate us into different castes and societies? I wanted to be free from all the obligations. I know that Sukhi would also come after me, and we would live happily. We shall come back to life after this, but we don't want to be part of these fake obligations of cruel society and blind people. So, I am giving up my life on my own and it has nothing to do with anyone."

Everyone was weeping bitterly for their loss, but Shilpa was not crying as she knew this might happen. When Monty came back and saw that Priya was also dead, he couldn't forgive himself. Shilpa was furious when he told her that he had shot Sukhi to death as well. Shilpa start to hit Monty for doing that; Monty was also crying and it seemed like he was also guilty for doing that. Shilpa then sobbingly went to Priya's mother and said that they could save their image and status in society and went away.

Mandy and Mike were standing next to Sukhi's body and crying for help. Sukhi breathed his last in the arms of his best friends. He stammered that they shouldn't hurt Monty for his actions. He knew that Priya was also coming with him to heaven and they were going to be very happy there. Mandy then shook his head and said he would kill Monty, but Sukhi held his hand and said they had to promise him that they would spare Monty and they agreed and then Sukhi lost his breath. Mike and Mandy had lost their friend, but they still hoped that Sukhi would rise again.

So, Sukhi and Priya gave up their life to live beyond the rules and regulations of this blind society. They gave up their love to be free from a cruel world – at last, they could be together and happy. They had faith in their love and didn't want to be part of this world of blind people who follow a mythical religious and caste system society, as ***love seeks no boundaries***.

IN THE AUTHOR'S WORDS:

Society is no different from us – we are a part of society. Society is not cruel, but we are all corrupted by the beliefs of our caste system or religion. Every religion has a different God and different rituals to follow. However, God created this world, and then He created human beings without any restrictions and obligations. If he looks at them now, he would be very disappointed that his children have strayed from the path of humanity and love.

In our society, there are some people who kill or hurt others in the name of God. They are just blindly following some myths about their religion or caste. There is nothing wrong in following religion, but instead of cutting another's hand, we have to extend our hands to help everyone.

No religion or caste teaches us to hate others – instead they taught us to love and help others. Everyone has the right to live their own lives and develop their own principles, but if they try to help others and love everyone, God will be happy and there will be no sorrow around us.

I hope Sukhi and Priya are still watching us from the heavens and are smiling down at us. They wanted to live but circumstances and fate was not on their side – now they are free from all the restrictions of society. They gave up their life to change the thinking of those around them.

I would like to ask my readers how they would react if they faced caste cruelty around them: Will you try to convince those around you, or will you also give up your life? But before making up your mind, remember that change will come if you can change yourself or at least your surroundings as a first step – then, you can expect the world to be fair to you. I wish you well, and hope that change will come soon.

Made in the USA
Middletown, DE
15 July 2025